T0208359

GLOBAL ONE

James P. Travers

ARCHWAY
PUBLISHING

Archway Publishing books may be ordered through booksellers or by contacting:

Archway Publishing
1663 Liberty Drive
Bloomington, IN 47403
www.archwaypublishing.com
1 (888) 242-5904

ISBN: 978-1-4808-4193-2 (sc)
ISBN: 978-1-4808-4194-9 (e)

Library of Congress Control Number: 2016921390

Print information available on the last page.

Archway Publishing rev. date: 1/6/2017

To all who helped me with this project,
especially Mom, Dad, and Carolyn.

I would like to take this opportunity to thank you, the reader, and say a few words. Throughout this book I use the points of view of many different characters. I change point of view often at chapter breaks as well as the beginning and end of chapters. If you are searching for an easy read, this may not be the book for you. It is not my intention to confuse you but to make you pause and think about each point of view of the characters. I encourage you to pause and reflect at chapter breaks and at the ends of the chapters.

While I concentrate on the two main characters, President Gunman and Dr. H, and their points of view, I introduce other characters throughout the story. My intent is not to frustrate you but to entertain and introduce a philosophical scenario. Should we as a civilization continue to act for the good of the many at the expense of the few? Or should we evolve and begin to think of the individual as an equal to the many?

I love my country and wish no harm to come to it, but the philosophic scenario does include a horrific catalyst that sets the main characters on their own philosophic adventures. I hope you enjoy the journey as much as I have in writing it. I look forward to continuing the main characters' journeys in the next book. I hope you will too.

CHAPTER 1

President Zachary Gunman glides out of the Oval Office and heads to the White House situation room. President Gunman was born in Virginia. He is average height, about five-foot-eleven. He has perfectly sculpted facial features with blond hair and blue eyes. He has a muscular build, more athletic in nature, not bulky like a weightlifter. He is a retired four-star general from the US Air Force.

It is now January 2025.

As I walk toward the situation room for the first official meeting, I have a mix of emotions—great moral responsibility with a touch of excitement and a little fear that I won't always get *it* right. I am about to conduct my first intelligence briefing as the most powerful man on earth.

However, the campaign process was a hard-fought battle. I made some enemies during that process. I hope they're not enemies who will do any harm to our country, but I have some reservations. I must be a powerful leader that resonates in my mind above all else.

I greet the chief of staff, Patrick Martin, my longtime friend and political confidant. Pat was a full colonel in the US Air Force who was in charge of the Fifty-Second Tactical Fighter Wing Intelligence Division at Spangdahlem Air Force Base in Germany.

After his retirement he was appointed assistant director of the CIA. He was the youngest person in the history of the CIA to achieve such a posting after his retirement. I have the utmost respect and confidence in his abilities.

I was going to choose him as my vice president at the Democratic National Convention, but my advisors correctly thought that in order to win the presidency, I needed to consolidate the Democratic Party and choose my rival during the campaign. My vice president is Bernie Sands. I do have great respect for the man, even though our views differ on specific aspects of government.

I break the silence and ask Pat, "Will Director Nichols be conducting the intelligence portion of the briefing this morning?"

Pat hesitates for a moment and then says, "No Zac."

"Did you inform Director Nichols that his presence was not optional, that it was mandatory?" I ask, annoyed at Pats's response.

"I did, Zac, and his resignation will be on your desk by the end of day. But of course, the proper congressional process will officially remove him," Pat responds.

"I was hopeful we could put aside our differences and work together. The man has valuable information and knowledge that would be useful, but I see that is not going to happen. Put together a short list of suitable men for the director's job. Prioritize it, and do it fast, Pat. I can count on your insight and experience in this area."

I note that Pat changed in an instant. A broad smile envelopes his face as he realizes the enormous power and responsibility he has as chief of staff. But I also note that he quickly erases any show emotion. He opens the door for me, and I enter the situation room.

I am instantly barraged by greetings of "Good morning, Mr. President," and a round of applause erupts from the select group. I nod with appreciation and say in a baritone voice, "Good morning, everyone. Let us begin."

Assistant Director Hush of the CIA begins to speak. "I would like to extend my apologies for the absence of Director Nichols. I will conduct the intelligence portion of the briefing, Mr. President, if that is acceptable."

"It is not acceptable, Mr. Hush, but proceed anyway," I say nonchalantly.

I know the main topic of the briefing typically concentrates on terrorist activity throughout the world. There are updates on the current involvement in Iraq, Syria, and other countries where US troops are operating, though the rest of the world is often led to believe operating in advisory roles only.

I interrupt Mr. Hush, and in an agitated voice, I say, "I have read everything you have told me so far—in newspapers and magazines over the holidays! I expected more from your office, Assistant Director. We are at war, gentlemen. This is a fight that has a front line on many shores as well as in the mountains. A war that never sees a dwindling number of people willing to sacrifice their lives for a cause. We must develop new plans and conduct more special operations—here at home and abroad. In order for us to achieve our goals, we must have the most current information available to us through our many different sources. Now go back to your office and research. I want to see you back in my office at 7:00 a.m. tomorrow. Do you understand, Mr. Hush?"

"Yes, sir, Mr. President," responds Hush as he collects his notes and puts them in his briefcase. He then makes a hasty exit.

"I want this information. Do I make myself clear on this?" I say with a look of disgust on my face.

Mr. Hush again responds, "Yes, sir," before the door quietly closes.

I feel it is necessary to express myself that nothing but the best will be accepted in this room from this day forward. I look directly to the commander of the joint chiefs of staff, Admiral Sheridan of the US Navy. "Commander, do you have any information for me that I need to know?" I ask in a firm but respectful voice.

"Mr. President, I know there are many items of information that you need to know about. I will start with our current naval deployments in the Middle East area of operations. Currently, we have a presence in—"

"Commander! I am more concerned with the current special operations that are being employed by the navy to combat the ever-growing terrorist threat that we face here at home and abroad," I say as I stare at him.

He looks away and down at his very thin stack of papers and says, "I don't have that information available at the moment, Mr. President."

"When do you think you'll have this information for me, Commander? I want that information by the end of the day, and I want preparations to begin to increase special operations. I want plans drawn up. I want estimates of how many troops will be needed. I want an intensive training program put in place to increase the number of special-op soldiers. Commander, do I make myself clear?"

Commander Sheridan simply responds, "Crystal clear, Mr. President."

"I will be waiting to hear from you, and Admiral, I *hate* waiting."

Without another spoken word, Admiral Sheridan hurriedly gets up and exits the briefing room.

I am infuriated at this point. *Who do these people think I am?* I begin to eyeball each and every one of the three remaining military members of the joint staff. I move my head slowly from one to the next, always maintaining eye contact. I take a deep breath and then speak, "Gentlemen, I truly believe this must be a joint effort. Does everyone understand? Be prepared by 7:00 a.m., or be prepared to be replaced. I think our briefing is done for the day."

The remaining men and women say, "Yes, Mr. President," and then they all prepare to leave. Within moments, the briefing room is empty except for Pat and me.

Pat says, "Well, Mr. President, you certainly know how to clear a room of the most powerful men and women in the world—apart from yourself, of course. Zac, I have a book in my office you might want to browse: *How to Make Friends and—*."

"All right, Pat. Very funny," I say, still angry about the briefing.

Pat replies, "I think you made some enemies."

"I didn't get elected to make friends. I'm going to serve this country to the best of my ability. I will not allow the bureaucrats and the bull-shitters to reside in this house."

"Yes, sir, Mr. President. Would you like me to fire anyone else today?"

"Don't brownnose me, Pat. You know I hate it when you do that."

"I'm just trying to lighten the mood about a thousand degrees. Actually, I am very impressed the way you handled yourself. A lesser man would have been in awe in those surroundings. Nope, not you. You sent them packing with a message," Pat says.

"I'm glad I have your approval, Pat, I don't know what I would do without you," I say, actually meaning ever word.

"Well, Zac, you would probably have a CIA director who showed up for briefings," Pat say with a smile.

"But seriously, Pat, I have a real sense of urgency when it comes to the worldwide terrorist threat. I am not just saying that to win votes and impress people. I mean, I really do think that our country needs to be more prepared. Everyone needs to act as if we are in a state of war. I'm not getting that feeling of a sense of urgency from our CIA and the joint chiefs.

"I want to be as prepared as we can. We live in the present but react to the future. I want this country to be prepared in the present to prevent acts of terror. I don't want to react to *it* when something does happen whatever the *it* may be. And Pat, have a short list for the CIA director on my desk in an hour."

"You got it, Zac," Pat said.

Pat rushes out the door, and I am left standing alone in the situation room. I have to pause and reflect for a moment. I want to be the president who puts an end to terrorism, not a president who contributes to increasing its grip over humanity. I want to be a president who can finally bring peace around the globe, one who can end the suffering of millions of innocent people. I know that these kinds of thoughts are idealistic. But I must face the challenges head-on. I know that I face many challenges at the present. Even if everyone in the world thinks that the challenges we face may be too great to overcome or even achieve, I must stay the course. I must stay the course not only outside the walls of the White House but especially within them. There is nothing that can deter me of my goals as president of these United States.

CHAPTER 2

Dr. Horatio Hornswoggle and his multimillion-dollar, customized Gulfstream Learjet make a perfect landing at Melbourne International Airport in Australia.

As my plane taxies to its private hangar, I think about how tired I feel and how I can't wait to get to my suite at the headquarters of StereoOpticon. My adrenalin kicks in after seeing the lights at Melbourne International Airport. It always does when I come home. I can feel it pulsing through my veins. I can feel the excitement starting to build on my return flight from China.

My pilot taxies the jet to a high-gloss black limousine waiting at hanger 13. I am thankful that I don't have to wait in the lines at airport customs. I am met by a customs agent as I exit the large twin-engine jet. After a few quick questions from the customs agent, I can slide into the backseat of my shiny limousine. My driver gently closes the door and moves behind the wheel of the large automobile. The chauffeur then drives the limousine toward StereoOpticon Communications.

I love the feeling of being pampered. "Why shouldn't I?" I say out loud.

My attentive personal assistant, Ms. Daly Waters, is in the backseat with me, and she says, "Excuse me, sir?"

"Ms. Waters, it's good to see you. Remind me to never go on

another trip without you. Can you do that for me?" I say, pointing at my back.

She begins to massages my back. She already has a cold beverage in a cup holder next to me. I gaze out the window and see lights flash by and realize what a lucky man I am. I have people around me who care and a successful company. I don't feel alone at all.

In what seems like an instant, I am overlooking the command and control center of the communications company. I walk closer to the window and see many people scrambling about like worker ants performing their required tasks. As I inspect my army of the most prized communication and information technology specialists in the world, I am reminded of the fact that I could never have achieved such success without everyone working as a team.

I am deep in thought about the recent launch of the fourth communications satellite from China's secret space station at Jiuquan near the Gobi Desert. I feel as though I am so close to completing a goal I have had for a long time.

Aided by the Chinese government, the launch was a resounding success. *Finally, I will become the richest man on the planet.* My advanced communications network is now a reality, or it will be very soon. Nothing can stand in my way of becoming the world's richest bachelor.

The silence is broken by Ms. Waters. "Shall I have your executive staff gather for the briefing now, sir?"

"Absolutely. Thank you, Ms. Waters," I respond politely.

I look around the executive office. A beautiful twelve-seat mahogany desk looks back at me. I need a bigger desk. I will soon have more executives than seats. I gaze at the finest art on the walls. The art seems to be saying to me, "You must do more. Don't rest. The world needs you now more than ever." My thoughts are interrupted by my executive staff entering the office. I reach out to each person as they enter the room, and I give them brief words of praise and further instructions for what will be a monumentally successful venture undertaken by the company. When everyone has settled in, I begin the meeting by outlining a timeline for setup and further testing of the fourth satellite in orbit. I reiterate the need to create the most modern and sophisticated communications satellite network in the world.

"Ladies and gentlemen, the entire network must be integrated and in full operation by the first Saturday in April. I cannot stress the importance of this deadline enough. All resources at our disposal will be made available in order to achieve our goals. Overtime is not only approved. It is mandatory. Are there any questions?"

No one spoke.

"Excellent! I've taken the liberty to cater a small reception in the next room. Please join me as we celebrate this momentous occasion of our fourth satellite in orbit, an occasion that will set us apart from all other communication companies. We are at the top, and I want to make it clear to all of you that this is where we will stay forever."

I make it very clear to all the top-level executives about the magnitude of meeting all the upcoming important deadlines. The success of the company will ultimately be measured by us meeting important government contracts for the promised upgrades to their communication networks.

I realize, as does the staff, that there are many challenges that lie ahead, and they must work hard if this company is to become the elite communications provider in the world. However, content for the moment and looking forward to the challenges of the future, the company will embark on its next adventures with great optimism.

I lead an elite staff of ten to a large and beautifully furnished conference room where a complete smorgasbord is waiting. Catering staff immediately mee them with hors d'oeuvres on sterling silver platters. Extra large prawns and sea scallops wrapped in gourmet streaky bacon complete with miniature gold forks are slowly circulated around the spacious executive board room.

Two bartenders are hard at work, mixing and pouring any beverage desired, serving the drinks in the world's finest crystal glasses with gold-plated rims. The main course consists of prime rib with an exquisite au jus on the side. Various seasonal vegetables steamed to perfection are also available. For dessert there are ten different cheeses from around the world and fresh seasonal fruits. The chocolate lovers can enjoy triple chocolate ice cream, black forest cake, chocolate cream pie, handmade miniature chocolates from Europe, and chocolate-covered strawberries. Bartenders serve fifty-year-old iced wine from Germany and Dom Perignon Champagne from France, making the whole experience a truly international event of the finest food and beverages.

The evening seems to quickly wind down as the late evening approaches. I stand and tap the champagne flute gently with a knife. A sudden hush falls over the room. I clear my throat and begin to speak, "I would like to first thank our fine catering staff for a job well done." Loud applause erupts and then quickly quiets down.

"Next I would like to congratulate all of you on your hard work up to this point. Our work will become much harder in the future, but I am confident that everyone in this room is up to the enormous challenges we face in the years to come. The rewards for your hard work and diligence will be beyond your expectations.

"Now with that being said, Ms. Waters will hand out assignments to our five executive heads, who will all accompany me on a very important trip the day after tomorrow. The rest of you know what is expected in my absence. Make the necessary assignments and schedule the meetings. I want this company running as smooth as glass in my absence."

Everyone says in unison, "Yes, sir."

"Then I will say good evening, everyone." I grab my laptop and files of paperwork and make my way toward the exit.

Applause begins to echo in the large conference room as I disappear through an en-suite door to my home, a lavish dwelling on the top floor of StereoOpticon.

I walk directly to the big-screen television and grab the remote control. I power it up and tune in to CNN. I then walk to the security control pad and raise the curtains to reveal an awe-inspiring view of the city of Melbourne far below my building complex.

I punch in another cod, and the walk-in safe door disengages with a hissing sound. I begin filing away important paperwork and retrieving the necessary papers for the next trip. Then I power up the laptop computer and check the status of the communications satellite network. After analyzing the information, I begin to enter commands to the fourth satellite. Confident with the results, I then power down the laptop and exit the walk-in safe. I imput another code, and the safe door closes and locks.

Exhaustion falls over my body, so I retreat to the shower room. I push a code on the shower room control panel, and my large walk-in shower comes to life. Twenty multifunctional shower jets begin to spray water in all different directions. After several moments the shower jets begin to erupt body wash, covering me in a soapy lather.

I am momentarily startled when I feel a soft sponge on my back. I do not need to turn around because I know who it is. It is my trusted personal assistant, Daly Waters. After several more moments, the shower jets spray clear water, and then the shower automatically shuts down. From the ceiling a high-powered fan begins to wind up and warm air begins to flow. Within minutes any trace of moisture is gone, and the fan begins to wind back down. I easily slide into my silk robe.

I break the silence and ask Ms. Waters, "Has everyone left for the evening?"

A soft voice speaks up and says, "The five executives leaving the day after tomorrow have decided to spend the night in the guest suites. They want to stay here to take care of the last-minute details before they depart."

I move slowly, feeling the energy drain from my body as I reach into my bedside refrigerator and grab a mineral water. I then stretch out on silk sheets to watch news updates on CNN. Ten silky smooth fingers begin to massage my feet and legs. The news cast quickly becomes only background noise as I fall into a deep sleep.

I wake up to a pleasant tone emanating from my watch, which is programmed to respond at 6:00 a.m. Within minutes a bell rings from my dumbwaiter, which delivers my hot breakfast and freshly brewed Colombian coffee. The kitchen staff members below are worth their weight in gold. I eat my breakfast slowly and listen to news updates again.

The news of the day reveals more instability in the Middle East. American soldiers are trying to squash uprisings in order to stabilize the region. I shake my head in disgust, knowing that innocent lives will be lost. But I realize the lives of those who are not so innocent will be lost as well.

I rest most of the day, knowing a brutal schedule is ahead of me. Ms. Waters handles the operations of the company with only limited interruptions.

The next day at precisely 7:00 a.m. a knock on the door interrupts my thoughts on global politics. Ms. Waters informs me that my helicopter is en route and will arrive within minutes to take us to Melbourne International Airport.

On the rooftop of StereoOpticon Communications, Ms.

Waters, Stewart Ballarat, Bill Feeney, Elizabeth Riley, Carolyn Cordero, John Detori, and I are ready to depart for China. As we take off, I am deep in thought. I know I have assembled the best team to make crucial communications upgrades.

The next three stops are the company's most important stops to date—Beijing, Moscow, and Washington, DC. Within minutes the helicopter begins its final approach into Melbourne International Airport. We make a perfect landing, and we're off on the next leg of our journey. A customs agent checks passports and clears us for the next leg of our journey.

As soon as everyone is on board, the pilot of my new Gulfstream executive-class Jet begins to taxi down the runway. Once the jet is at cruising altitude, my staff and I are served morning beverages and a light breakfast. I inform my staff of their tasks and the timetables that we must meet. I make a point to emphasize that the timetable for the projects must be precise. I also go over some crucial procedures for the installation of the communications networks.

The first stop is Beijing. Bill Feeney and Elizabeth Riley will remain in China to install the necessary upgrades within the communications networks and bring the Chinese to another level. Within moments of the conclusion of the staff meetings, the pilot informs the passengers over the intercom to prepare for landing at Beijing International Airport.

The pilot makes a perfect landing and taxis to the appropriate gate. Mr. Feeney and Ms. Riley, who both speak fluent Chinese and are experts in communications, gather their belongings. They disembark the aircraft, and they are quickly ushered to a waiting black sedan where two representatives from the Chinese government will escort them to their work sites.

The plane then taxis to a hangar for refueling. When we disembark, security checks our passports, and we board another one of my planes with fresh pilots and crew members. Within thirty minutes, the pilot has the crew and passengers airborne again. We are headed for Moscow this time with an estimated arrival time of about eight hours.

Once again at cruising altitude, I have the crew serve cocktails and then prepare the evening meal. The passengers make themselves comfortable in their own seats. The business of the day has finally come to a conclusion.

In the meantime, I have retreated to my personal cabin. It is a small space but well-stocked with necessities. I finish my meal and then open my laptop to check on the progress of my employees. The integration of the new satellite seems flawless. I relay some messages to my teams in Australia on a job well done. I am very happy with the results. I turn off my laptop, store it in my safe, and then retire to a comfortable bed for some well-deserved rest.

I wake up about an hour before arrival. I retreat to the small but comfortable washroom facilities to freshen up before our arrival in Moscow. I return to my private quarters, where the staff serves my breakfast—chilled fruit cocktail, French toast with cinnamon and maple syrup, pineapple juice, and freshly brewed coffee from Columbia.

After breakfast I take my laptop out of the safe and check that the operating system of my communications company is ready to enable the multiple systems coming online. Confident of the work done up to this point, my attention shifts as the plane begins its descent into Moscow. I look out of a small window to view the landscape below. The unique architecture of the buildings soon comes into focus as the plane descends. The size of the rooftops grows out of the white blanket of snow.

The Moscow skyline has its own grandeur unlike any other place in the world. Rising out of the barren lands are spectacular glowing gold domes with long and fat toothpick points everywhere, pointing to the sky. The high towers that hold the brilliant gold domes are a milky white with arc windows scattered generously around them. The white buildings make up a surreal skyline that is surpassed by no other city on earth. However, there are few skyscrapers that conflict with the beauty of the ancient architecture.

As the plane descends, I see St. Basil's Cathedral, which was finished in 1561. It is the true expression of the history of Moscow. How it has survived through the turbulent periods of Moscow's past is a tribute to its beauty. Each dome is slightly a different shape, size, and color. The centerpiece of the building is a crown that tapers off to a gradual peek. It reminds me of a needle balancing above the gorgeous monstrosity.

The best things in life are the small achievements that may be easy to miss. There is beauty in every level of the cathedral, but it is a triumph of the human spirit when the little things in life can rise above and tower over all else. The small steps that mankind has taken deserve the most credit for our existence. I am overcome with inspiration. I realize at that moment I want to become a humanitarian and use my wealth for the betterment of mankind.

This cathedral is one of mankind's crowning achievements, and it is belittled by the fantastic advancements that actually define our existence in the present. One small step for man can really turn into one gigantic leap for mankind. This cathedral has existed for so long, and it embodies the true attributes that mankind has to offer the future.

Within seconds the plane gently touches the runway, and the engines throttle higher as the plane slows down. I close my laptop and store it in my hidden safe. The captain and copilot have certainly earned a rest. Thankfuly, their journey is now complete.

I am happy to see the Russian representatives waiting for us. Four Russian government representatives meet us at the gate with two shiny black sedans. They quickly lead us into the sedans, and then we are en route to the Kremlin in the heart of the city. One of the Russians informs us that no weapons are allowed and that we must turn over any on our person at once. I inform them that no one is carrying any weapons. He seems content with my response, and he doesn't say another word.

The temperature in the vehicle was very comfortable, but as we exit, everyone is hit with a chilly gust of wind. We hurry to the the main doors to avoid the cold.

Everyone squeezes into the elevator, and we are taken down several levels to the living quarters, where my two executives will spend as much time as needed until the communication upgrades are complete.

We are told that a briefing is scheduled in thirty minutes. No one is to leave their rooms until they are called. In the meantime, we are taken to our rooms. I decide to shower and put on a fresh suit. I then drink some bottled water to fight the dehydration from the flights.

Everyone is ushered into the hallway. I will meet with the Russian president, Saratog Volochek, in about thirty minutes. Carolyn Cordero, John Detori, Stuart Ballarat, Ms. Waters, and I are led into a small conference room where an English interpreter explains the rules and hands out badges that we must wear at all times. After brief instructions, we are led on a brief tour of the secret facilities where the communication upgrades will take place.

I am excited about the scheduled meeting with the Russian president. I am escorted into an elaborately furnished office where the Saratog Volochek is patiently waiting. I take a seat in front of the massive dark redwood desk covered with papers, Russian knickknacks, and a large bottle of Russian vodka. President Volochek extends his hand out, and I give him a very firm handshake. The president then reaches for two glasses and pours a large amount of the clear liquid. Without speaking a word, he offers a glass to me with only a nod of his head.

The president raises his glass and looks me straight in the eyes and finally speaks, "Here's to your health," he says with a Russian accent. He then lets out a deep laugh that bounces off the walls before it dies out into silence. We raise our glasses and take a mouthful of the clear liquid.

"How long for communication upgrade?" President Volochek asks.

I can tell the president doesn't speak English that well. I decide to speak slowly while enunciating each word to make the meeting go more smoothly. "The process demands that the whole communications network be shut down for a period of time and new software initiated in its place. It must then be coordinated with the rest of the communications network throughout the country. The work will be carried out by two of my most elite communication experts, Ms. Cordero and Mr. Detori, who both speak fluent Russian as well. The exact timetable is hard to predict. One month has been allocated for this procedure. As more time passes, a more exact estimate will be given to you. Does this meet with your approval, Mr. President?"

"This is acceptable. The time that the communication system is shut down must be approved by only me. It must be short in duration. The reasons are for national security. You must realize," said the president.

"Of course, Mr. President. I will inform my people of your request, and I assure you that we will strictly adhere to your request."

"In addition, I wish to remind you that all systems within the network must remain top secret and never revealed to anyone ever ... under any circumstances," said the president.

The president's English has improved dramatically, it seems.

"Yes, Mr. President, you have my word as a gentleman and a scholar that no information will be made available to anyone outside my circle of top executives."

A broad smile stretches across president's face. "Then we drink to our concluded bargain. Your payment will be deposited into your bank account at the conclusion of a successful test of the new system. Agreed?"

I say, "Agreed."

We finish what's left in our glasses, and President Volochek refills the glasses once more.

President Volochek breaks the silence. "How long will you be staying as our guest?"

It feels like the mood just got a lot softer. "It is regretful, but I must leave at first light tomorrow morning."

"Then you must join me for dinner this evening. I will have the chef prepare something special in your honor. How does 6:00 p.m. sound?"

"That is very kind of you, Mr. President. I look forward to the opportunity to sample Russian cuisine."

"Wonderful. I regret that the affairs of the state are calling me back to duty. You must excuse me now." The president raises his glass, and both of us drain what is left of the vodka.

I stand, feeling a bit wobbly from the rapid succession of drinks, and then I say, "Until this evening then."

A chaperone almost instantly escorts back to my temporary living quarters. I am drawn to my bed like iron to a magnet. I feel very tired and sleepy. I decide to rest before dinner.

I am awoken by several knocks on my door. I look at my watch, and I realize it is 5:00 p.m. already. When I raise my head, it feels as if it has been hit by a hammer. I slowly walk to the door and open it enough to peer through the crack to see my personal assistant, Ms. Waters.

I step to the side and open the door enough to let her in. She sidesteps the door and looks at me. She opens her bag and gives him two white pills. I take them, thank her, and offer her a seat by gesturing to the nearest chair. She obligingly sits as I turn to retrieve a bottle of water from the small wet bar. I immediately put the pills in my mouth and consume the entire bottle of water.

I say, "I needed that."

Ms. Waters smiles and responds, "Is there anything else I can do for you?"

The look on her face is that of a subtle smile of joy mixed with willing submission. I stare for a moment, and then it's as if I am seeing her for the first time. I realize that I want her for more than just an assistant.

Her strawberry locks fall delicately over her shoulders, and she brushes her wavy hair back slightly to reveal the olive color of her face. Her stunning green eyes have thin streaks of gold that run through them like small rivers leading to clear white boundaries. Her eyebrows are thin and well cared for. They match her hair perfectly, and they also contrast remarkably well with her eye color.

She has high cheekbones that required very little makeup. Her mouth is small, yet her lips are full. She seems too tall in high heels, but her actual height is just under six feet. She wears a tight-fitting pinstripe skirt well above her knees.

Her legs have the shape of a gymnastics athlete's. She has a flat stomach covered by a matching suit coat that gives her an air of professionalism and feminine appeal. Her chest is ample, yet her clothing leaves much to the imagination.

Regretfully, I have to say, "No, thank you. I'm having dinner with the president, and I must get ready."

Precisely at 6:00 p.m. I hear a knock on the door. I open the door to see my familiar chaperone again. He's an older gentleman dressed in a black suit and tie. The gentleman holds out his hands in a gesture that says I should follow him now. So I follow him without speaking.

He leads me into a grand dining room beautifully furnished with antiques. On either end of the room, there is a large fireplace. Someone had constructed it with beautifully polished stone masonry. The flames makes a triangle of yellows, reds, and blues that provide adequate heat. Along the walls, there are portraits of every czar in Russian history as well as the more current leaders, including Stalin, Lennon, Gorbachov, and Putin.

I take in the remarkable furnishings, and I notice that there is a large chandelier hanging above the dining table. It is crafted with various sizes of crystal that reflects the bright light, making each a kaleidoscope that is quite hypnotic.

I note that the mahogany dining table seats at least twenty-two people comfortably. The handcrafted chairs match the set too, and they look as if they were made in the nineteen century. The chairs are accented by hand-carved circular designs covering the entire chair down to the legs. It seems a bit much for just the two of us, but I enjoy every moment of the lavish surroundings.

I'll surely enjoy the meal, whatever it is, in this setting. The meal turns out to be a classic Russian cuisine. Borscht is served first.

I say, "Mr. President, I have never had borscht. It is very good. My compliments to the chef."

"I will tell him you enjoyed his borscht," says the president.

I am thrilled with the main course, which consists of beef stroganoff. The after-dinner course consists of an elaborate display of fine cheeses, and it is accompanied by Russian champagne, which is incredibly delicious when it's served very cold. The staff also serves chilled Russian vodka with a hint of cherry flavor, which I think complements the vodka taste.

I'm thrilled that some of Russia's most talented violinists play flawless music after dinner. *What a delightful evening.*

After everyone clears the room, President Volochek says, "If the communications system fails or is compromised by anyone, there will be no place on earth that you can hide. Do I make myself clear?"

I realize the tone of the evening has shifted. I respond, "Mr. President, I can assure you of the success of this communication upgrade and the utmost confidentiality that will accompany it. If there is a need to do any follow-up work on your communication network, I will personally see to it myself. I will not be in hiding. I can assure you of that."

"Very good. That is exactly what I wanted to hear from you. I wish you a pleasant journey tomorrow," the president says.

"Thank you, and I will remain in close contact with you, Mr. President," I say in response.

I'm then escorted back to my room by my familiar but unspeaking chaperone. I feel a burning sensation in my eyes, and I know sleep is not far away. I undress and go immediately to bed. Before I fall asleep, I set my watch for 6:00 a.m. Russian time.

A little jingle emanates from my watch seemingly instantaneously. I quickly shower, dress, and gather my belongings. I open the door and wander into the hallway. One of the Russian chaperones meets my gaze at the end of the hall but offers no smile. I stop at the next door and knock lightly.

Ms. Waters opens the door and invites me in with a gesture of her hand and a smile.

"The pilots have sent word that the plane is ready when you are," she says.

I pick up her fine cashmere coat and hold it out for her. "The car is ready and waiting," she says in a most professional manner.

"Excellent," I say.

We walk out of the room and down the hall to the waiting escort. Ms. Waters follows closely behind. We are soon met by Stewart Ballarat.

The ride to the airport is uneventful, but there's a lovely sunrise with light pink streaks with orange and yellow shooting out in all directions when we arrive. As I board the plane, I think, *What a perfect complement to a successful trip to Moscow.*

My thoughts quickly turn to our next destination, Washington, DC. Within minutes the plane is racing down the runway for a perfect takeoff and a long hop across the pond. I figure we'll land in about twelve hours, the maximum flight time for this aircraft.

After breakfast Stewart Ballarat and I begin another conference to assure a smooth transition of the upgraded communications software in in the United States. The network for the US government is by far the most complicated and difficult upgrade that the team has ever faced to date.

I am very confident with my most accomplished executive and right-hand man, Stewart Ballarat. We plan to personally perform the required tasks to upgrade the US communication system.

We end up spending most of the twelve-hour flight in conference, allowing for meal breaks and coffee breaks and little else. The flight passes quickly because of the amount of information and complex programs that we need to discuss. The pilot announces our arrival at the Reagan International Airport outside of Washington, DC.

The plane begins its descent, and I gather my paperwork and my laptop and put them in a briefcase. I then buckle in for the landing. I feel confident that everything will go well for the most important encounter of my life, the meeting with President Gunman.

At that moment I begin to feel the jet rock from side to side and sway up and down abruptly. The pilot announces that we may encounter additional turbulence because of an approaching storm moving northeast up the coast. These types of storms usually bring high winds with them, but they are often short in duration.

The plane shifts and lurches from side to side, the turbulence increasing in intensity. The whole plane begins to shake vigorously. It feels like a great force of wind grabs the plane and raises us several hundred meters up and to the right. Then the plane dives in a steep descent.

The pilot makes some quick adjustments and pulls the nose up with only moments to spare before the approach. He stabilizes the plane, and the wheels touch down and then bounce off the tarmac and touch down again. The pilot quickly reverses the engines, slowing the jet down. With little runway to spare, the plane makes a 180-degree turn and heads toward the customs and unloading area.

This is not a good start to the biggest and most important contract my company will ever handle.

The plane eventually comes to a stop. A shiny black SUV is waiting for us nearby. A customs official hastily makes his way out to greet us and ask a few questions. When he asks if we have anything to declare, I say, "Yes, I have the best pilots in the world."

The customs official has a blank look on his face, trying to ascertain the meaning of the comment. It's obvious that he never will.

"Nothing to declare," I added.

The rest of the flight crew is questioned as well, and the satisfied official turns and walks away, confident of a job well done.

I'm then greeted by a serious-looking US government official, and we are escorted to a black SUV. Stewart Ballarat, Ms. Waters, and I get in the backseat. We immediately check for a strong but refreshing beverage to calm our nerves a bit from the landing.

We find a large bottle of single malt scotch, and we all enjoy a large glass diluted with water and ice. The calming effects of the expensive scotch make the rush-hour traffic delays seem tolerable as the large vehicle slowly snakes its way to the entrance gates of the White House. They ask us if we have any weapons. Of course, we don't.

An attentive US Marine serving as the security guard clears the SUV and its occupants. We are then processed into the White House and given badges to wear at all times on the premises. Secret Service then escorts us to our sleeping quarters.

I'm given the Lincoln room to sleep in. The walls are covered with pictures of the former president Abraham Lincoln. The room is also filled with Civil War memorabilia and a framed copy the Emancipation Declaration. There are other famous speeches perfectly framed that Lincoln had written himself during a period of great gloom in American history. Guests of the White House even use the same bed that Lincoln slept in. I feel right at home in this room.

Within moments of my arrival in the Lincoln Room, I am told by the president's secretary that the president is too busy to meet with me immediately. But I am invited for dinner that evening at 7:00 p.m.

I take the time available to unpack the necessary software that I'll need for the visit at the White House. I will have to install some of the communications software at the command and control center located in the White House. Additional software will also need to be installed at the alternate command center at the North American Aerospace Defense Command (NORAD). NORAD conducts aerospace warning, aerospace control, and maritime warning in the defense of North America. The Cheyenne Mountain Complex is a military installation and nuclear bunker located in Colorado Springs. Peterson Air Force Base is also located in Colorado Springs, where NORAD and the US Northern Command (USNORTHCOM) are headquartered. After all the installs are complete, the system will be linked throughout the entire United States.

Initially, the communication links will include government installations and agencies only. The communication upgrades will be able to withstand an electomagnetic pulse or (EMP) generated by a nuclear blast. Effectively, we will not lose communications in the event of a nuclear explosion.

We will ultimately make a version of the original programe available to businesses and finally private individuals. The future success of StereoOpticon rests heavily on the timely completion of the upgrades. More importantly, the software must deliver the promised results.

The current communications network used by the United States government has several weaknesses, which became apparent after the attack on the Twin Towers in New York City. The attack shut down communication avenues that affected reliable communications between government agencies. There were no nuclear explosions during that attack, and communications still failed.

At 6:30 p.m., my watch begins a little jingle of "Yankee Doodle Dandy". I know it's time to freshen up and dress for the business dinner with President Gunmen. I gaze into the mirror in the brightly lit bathroom to check my appearance. I want to make a good first impression with the president. I feel nervous, but I'm content with my appearance.

I exit the washroom and move to the wet bar and pour myself a single malt scotch to drink in order to calm my nerves a bit more. *Was it the landing at the airport, or is it the meeting with the president that has me nervous?* I try to dismiss both and concentrate on why I am here.

Just as I finish the last swallow of scotch, I hear a light rap on the door. I gather my paperwork and put it all in my black leather briefcase. I'm escorted to a small room on the second floor of the White House and invited to sit at the dining table, which has been set for just two people. A well-groomed White Jouse waiter almost immediately asks me if I'd like a beverage. And I say, "Scotch please. Thank you." The waiter then tells that the president will be along momentarily by the attentive waiter.

My nervousness is soon masked by two helpings of scotch. When the president enters the room, I stand up and hold out my hand. I give the president a firm handshake, maybe a little too firm, but we greet each other pleasantly.

I say, "It's an honor to meet you, Mr. President, and please call me Harry."

"Thank you, Harry," the president says with a slight smile on his face.

***

As I sit down, not taking my eyes off Harry, I am struck by his appearance. He is a tall man, about six-foot-four. His hair is the color of brown sugar. He has blue eyes. He is quite tan. His suit is impeccable, definitely a high-quality one. He certainly looks the part. He has the look of a man I can trust. I view this partnership as a technological advancement necessary for the future of the national security of the United States.

"On to more current matters. I have taken the liberty of selecting a lovely burgundy. It is a grand cru from Château Margo in east central France. It will go nicely with the chateaubriand the chef is preparing for us," I say.

"Oh, yes, it sounds like a perfect pairing. Thank you, Mr. President," Harry says without hesitation.

I continue, "Did you know that this dish is named after the French writer and statesman Francois-Rene Vicomte de

Chateaubriand. His chef is said to have created the dish. Isn't it odd that sometimes the one who creates something never gets the credit one deserves?"

"That is a fine analogy, Mr. President. Unfortunately, that type of thing has occurred since the dawn of mankind and will probably continue until the day mankind becomes extinct," Harry says.

I respond, "On the other side of the coin, some people do not want to take credit or responsibility for something they have done."

"That is true. However, some people want to take credit for their actions even if their actions lead to horrible endings. For example, leaders of terrorist organizations claim credit for attacks on innocent men, women, and children," Harry says.

"Wouldn't it be a political utopia if everyone acknowledged responsibility for what they have done and rejected responsibility for what they had no part in doing?"

"It is a grandiose idea, Mr. President," Harry says. He then continues after a short pause, "Mr. President, I would like to change the subject if I may and brief you on the communication upgrades. I will be overseeing the whole operation to ensure your complete satisfaction. My most elite executive, Stewart Ballarat, will be conducting most of the technical work necessary during installation. I would be glad to meet with you at any time during the entire process to update you on our progress. Is this acceptable to you, Mr. President?"

"That's fine. However, I will need to know in advance if parts of the system will be off-line and for how long in order to make the proper arrangements. It is vital that communications remain active in some form for national security reasons, of course."

"Of course Mr. President. I will keep you updated at all times, and if there are any other concerns, please let me know immediately," Harry says in a confident tone.

"I certainly will. Here's to a successful mission and under the strictest of confidentiality as well," I say as I raise my glass for a toast.

"Cheers! As you would say in America," Harry responds.

At that moment the waiter brings in the salads and a large appetizer of stuffed mushrooms. I ask, "Shall we eat?"

With a smile, Harry says, "Absolutely. I'm famished."

CHAPTER 3

The upgrades in the Unites States take more than sixty days. It's now April. I'm ecstatic to finally finish the business in the United States. The president and I have gotten along famously throughout the time period. The tests are all complete now. The upgrades have been achieved without any glitches.

In fact, all the upgrades are now finished in China and Russia too. All my executives are back at StereoOpticon. It is 7:00 a.m., and Mr. Ballarat, Ms. Waters, and I have just buckled our seatbelts for takeoff from Peterson Air Force Base in Colorado Springs. We are headed to Hawaii to refuel, and then we will continue on to Melbourne International Airport.

After many successful tests, the communications network is now integrated with the satellites, and everything is in working order. The upgrades and integration were completed right on schedule, and everyone is in a jovial mood, even though they're exhausted from their efforts over the past month. It has been a monumental achievement for StereoOpticon and the entire staff. Promotions and salary increases are ahead for everyone involved.

It is also the day when President Gunman will present his State of the Union address at the House of Representatives on Capitol Hill. One hundred days have passed since he took office. I'm very proud that we concluded our business in time. Almost all of the congressional members will be present for the speech, which will be aired live throughout the world. I'm hopeful that the president will mention something about the communication upgrades. But I also know there are national security issues at stake, so the likelihood of that happening is small. I still hold out some hope.

Our landing in Hawaii is uneventful. We all stay on board while refueling was underway. Within an hour we are ready for takeoff again with a fresh pilot. The Hawaiian Islands are spectacular to see on a sunny day. Unfortunately, there's a low cloud covering much of the islands.

It's just about time for the president's address, so I retreat to my personal cabin to watch and listen to his speech.

***

CNN has reported to its audience that there has been a change in policy. The vice president will not sit next to the speaker of the House as tradition dictates, but instead he will watch the speech from the comfort of the White House because of security reasons.

At approximately 8:00 p.m., Pat enters the Oval Office to inform me that it is time to leave. The ride to Capitol Hill is uneventful as the motorcade convoy speeds through downtown Washington, DC.

I read over the speech one last time. Within minutes we arrive at the Capitol Building. My entourage make their way to the entrance of the House floor and patiently wait behind closed doors for the traditional introduction.

The huge double doors to the House of Representatives are opened, and I hear a loud voice echoing throughout the chambers.

"Mr. Speaker, the president of the United States."

I feel a chill rise up my spine as I enter the chamber to thunderous applause. I shake hands with those on the aisle seats and make my way to the podium. The huge round of applause continues while I take in the whole atmosphere. I reach the podium, unable to hide a proud grin. I stand for several long moments as the clapping slowly dies down.

I begin, "Thank you, Mr. Speaker, members of the Senate and House of Representatives, and good evening to you, my fellow Americans. Tonight I would like to speak to everyone about the state of the union. It has been one hundred days since I took office. In that short period of time, my administration has made several historic achievements that have furthered the national security of our United States and the security of our allies around the globe."

**

Captain Benjamin Holt has just begun his shift as one of two officers on duty at the Twentieth Air Force, Ninety-First Space Wing at Minot Air Force Base in Minot, North Dakota. The other officer on duty is Captain Wheeler.

I say to Wheeler, "Where have you been? You're ten minutes late for your shift."

Wheeler responds, "Very funny, Holt. The one time you beat me into work all year. Boy, it's really coming down out there. I think we got about eight inches already."

"I thought you would get a kick out of that one. The other two wanted to go home early, so I came in to relieve them. Okay, let's start our systems check.

I take my place in front of several large computer screens. The day shift didn't report any problems. "Hey, Wheeler, what did you do?"

Wheeler responds, "What are you talking—"

I get the initial warning light, and within seconds at

approximately 7:15 p.m. central time, alarms and "launch in progress" indicators begin to sound off.

I look up and see that the launch doors to the silo have been activated and that the missile inside has begun the first stage of initiation for takeoff. I am stunned at first, wondering what we should do. Then my training takes over. I try to close the silo doors first, and when that doesn't work, I know that we have a serious problem.

I begin to yell, "Wheeler, get on the secure phone line to the EC-135 crew and ask them if they have control of a missile launch from here." I know the EC-135 Airborne Launch Control Aircraft takes control of the missile once it is launched. Surely, they would have prior knowledge of any launch.

Within moments Wheeler relays the message. "Holt, they have no prior knowledge of any launch. They are getting the same warnings as we are."

"Wheeler, let's try to shut the missile launch sequence down before it's too late. I already tried to close the silo bay doors. They won't close."

"Roger that!" says Wheeler.

I yell, "I'm trying everything I know to take the missile off-line. Nothing is working. Get back on the secure line and alert the EC-135 of our situation, and hurry!"

Wheeler responds, "Yes, sir!"

I hope the EC-135 can take over the guidance system of the missile once it has launched. I am moving at a frantic pace, punching in commands to prevent the missile launch. I yell again, "The commands aren't working! "Wheeler, I can now confirm the launch of one LGM-30 Minuteman III. Ask the EC-135 to confirm launch and ask them if they have control of the missile guidance system."

I know that no presidential order has been given to launch

the missile because I would have to verify the launch codes and activate the launch. I yell to Wheeler, "I am tracking the missile flight path!" In the event of an unauthorized launch and failure of primary protocol to stop the launch, secondary protocols are put into action. I yell to Wheeler again, "I'm calling the nearby surface-to-air missile station. They must have this missile on their radar. Wheeler, does the EC-135 have control?"

Wheeler yells back, "Negative! The EC-135 has no control."

I get on the phone with the surface-to-air missile squadron, and I tell them we have a rogue missile launch. I yell, "Yes, that's correct. Fire at will!" I hang up the phone and quickly realize the gravity of the situation. I then dial the number that no one wants to dial in a situation like this. I dial the president of the United States. I wait for what seems forever until I hear a voice on the other end of the line. I begin, "This is Captain Holt of the Ninety-First out of Minot. We have a rogue missile launch. I am tracking the path of a Minuteman III missile, and it is on a flight path toward Washington, DC. Do you copy?" I wait for a response. I look to my right and see that Wheeler is already talking to Vice-President Sands as protocol dictates.

***

I hear a ringtone emanating from my pocket. I reach into my suit pocket and pull out the president's phone, which I hold at all times when not in use. *Who could be calling the president in the middle of his speech?* I answer, "Hello, who is calling please?" I'm in disbelief at first. I imagine that it's a crank call. Then by the end of Captain Holt's message, I know it was real. I don't hesitate for a moment. I yell to the Secret Servicemen, "Get the president downstairs and in the hardened bunker. Do it now!"

I turn to the president and yell as loud as I can, "Mr. President, the speech is over. We must go now! Three Secret Servicemen are just about to grab the president. I yell again, "We must go now! Hurry, Mr. President!"

I see the Secret Servicemen practically scoop the president up and whisk him away from the podium. The crowd of US politicians are stunned into silence for a moment. I start heading toward the side door, which leads to an elevator that goes directly to the hardened shelter. By the time I get to the door, I can hear a multitude of ringtones getting louder by the moment. By the time the president, three servicemen, and I go through the doors, I can hear panic start to set in on the floor of the House of Representatives."

There is no time to think, only act. In the elevator, heading down to the bunker, the president says, "Pat? Are you out of your mind? What the hell is going on?"

I look at the elevator lights blink. Every second seems like a minute. I look at the president and say, "Mr. President, we have to get to the hardened bunker immediately. I will explain when you are safe inside."

"Damn it, Pat. You will tell me now!" the president says with a mixture of confusion and anger.

I am about to begin my explanation when the elevator door opens. The Secret Servicemen, doing what they are trained to do, grab the president and head straight for the blast doors. I move as fast as possible behind the president. When we are in the bunker, I push the door shut. I hit the mechanism to vacuum seal the bunker. My only thought at that moment is, *The president is safe.*

***

"Pat, there could only be one reason why we are in this bunker," I say. I look at Pat square in the eyes, glance over his shoulder, and see the head of the Secret Service, Mr. Pringle, booting up the satellite communications. Then I glance back at Pat.

"Yes, sir, Mr. President. There is a single Minuteman III that launched from Minot, and the flight path indicated it was headed straight for Washington, DC. I'm sure the vice president and the first lady have been notified by now."

"All right, Pat, let's make sure Vice-President Sands and Carol have been notified." I look over Pat's shoulder again and make eye contact with Mr. Pringle. He nods his head as if he can read my mind. I look back at Pat, who is almost not willing to accept what is happening. "Assuming you're correct about the missile's flight path and intended target, how much time do we have?"

"Well, I've been thinking about that. The missile will hit its ceiling at seven hundred miles above Earth and at twenty-four times the speed of sound. Subtracting the time it took for notification and the time get here, I would say we will know in ninety seconds.

"All right, Pat, let's get to work. I know we haven't had much practice at this, but let's get it right the first time. You take the tracking computer and keep me updated. I'll get our defenses up and running. Let's see if we can knock this thing out of the sky and into the ocean."

I enter my access codes into the central computer. Within moments all the computers in the command center light up. I enter more commands to take complete control of the air defenses. "Pat, do you have the missile on your tracking computer?"

Pat immediately responds, "Acquiring track, still acquiring, still acquiring. Got it, Zac. I'm relaying the missile track over to you now. Thirty-five seconds until target. I can confirm missile decent at twenty-four times the speed of sound. Zac, we have another launch out of Minot. Just came up on the tracking radar."

"Copy that. Let's get this one. Initiating lock-on sequence and automatic air defense firing status. Come on. Lock on. Lock on. Got it! Automatic firing on green light. Come on. Come on. Missile impact in ten seconds. Switching to manual air defense firing status. All missiles away! Impact in three, two, one. Impact."

I listen and wait and watch my computer screen flicker and then die out. I suddenly feel a slight tremor under my feet.

Pat breaks the silence. "I can confirm nuclear detonation. We are at ground zero."

"Let's get the radiation suits on, gentlemen. Mr. Pringle, will you assist Mr. Marshall and Mr. Feller with their suits? Pat, get your suit on. We have more work to do, much more."

CHAPTER 4

'm awoken by his cell phone ringing on his nightstand. It is the middle of the night in Moscow. I listen in disbelief. I say, "On my way!"

Could this really be happening? A nuclear explosion in Washington, DC? As I finish my thought, I hear a loud knock on my door, and my three body guards come rushing in to protect me. I quickly finish dressing and hustle down to the secure bunker deep beneath the Kremlin.

Once safely inside my own bunker in Russia's command center, I am briefed on the situation at hand. The command center computer technology has confirmed one nuclear blast in the heart of Washington, DC.

I look at the infrared signature computer and see that another nuclear missile is en route. One Minuteman III nuclear warhead with a single reentry warhead, I hope. *I hope the United States has kept their promise to refit all its nuclear missiles with single-entry warheads only as we have done in January 2020.*

I track the missile on the computer and see it is flying at about seven hundred miles above the Earth at a high rate of speed. *There is no way to shoot the warhead down at that altitude and speed.* It is currently over the North Atlantic Ocean on a heading that makes its final destination had to predict. I am told the missiles originated from the United States.

I look to the two officers on duty, Lieutenant Puletski and Captain Kopetski. I ask Captain Kopetski, "Have you initiated the call roster to have my cabinet members come in immediately, Captain"?

He responds, "Yes, sir."

I ask him if we are in contact with the American ambassador at the embassy in Moscow.

"Yes, sir."

I realize I have very few minutes to analyze the situation and retaliate if necessary. It's odd that the Americans would launch an unprovoked nuclear missile at Moscow and even more strange to detonate one over Washington, DC. Therefore, I conclude that the missile launch was unintentional. However, the reality of the situation threatens Moscow. I direct my question to Captain Kopetski again, "What does the American ambassador say?"

"He is unable to contact the president or the vice president at the moment, but he is still trying," he says calmly. "He assures us that the United States has not intentionally launched a nuclear missile. Mr. President, should we retaliate in kind to this unprovoked attack?"

I respond immediately, "We must not escalate this situation into a full-scale nuclear war."

I keep an eye on the tracking information and see the missile is about one minute outside of Holland's airspace. I seize the opportunity to test the new communication upgrades. "I give the order to launch one nuclear missile and aim it at Washington, DC," the president says calmly.

A confused look appears on Captain Kopetski's face. "Washington, DC, is already destroyed, Mr. President," he responds.

"I have the launch codes, Captain. Enter them into the computer," I say, handing them over. "And Captain, do not question me again."

"Yes, Mr. President," Kopetski responds. "The codes are entered into the computer, and the launch has been initiated."

"Can we confirm launch?" I ask.

"Negative, Mr. President. No launch has occurred," Kopetski says with a confused look on his face. "I see the missile has changed course and is now heading southeast toward Rome."

"Mr. Kopetski, run a check on our launch system and find out if there is a malfunction immediately," I say.

"Right away, sir."

I continue to attempt to launch a retaliatory missile and continue to track the in-flight missile bound for Rome. I look on the computer to see where the missile is tracking. I view potential targets on the missile's current flight path. As the list appears, it becomes glaringly evident where the nuclear missile will strike.

At this point the missile is nearing its maximum range. If it continues on its current heading and flies over Athens, there can be only one target left.

The missile flies over Athens and begins its descent toward one of the holiest places on earth. Tel Aviv in Israel is the only remaining target. I know the Israeli officials have been notified and have also been tracking the missile with their early warning and detection radars. I also know sirens have been activated, warning citizens to take shelter. I can see on the computer the infrared signals from all of Israel's Patriot missile systems being launched in an attempt to shoot the missile down or at least knock it off course into the Mediterranean Sea.

Even I know the newly upgraded surface-to-air Patriot missile system was designed to shoot down aircraft and not high-speed incoming nuclear missiles. But I wait to see if they can knock the missile off course. Then I see a nuclear expulsion detected at 3:45 a.m. on my computer. Ground zero seems to be over the Mediterranean, just to the west of Israel .

Was the maximum range of the nuclear missile hit, or did the surface-to-air missile system knock the missile off course? And why didn't our nuclear missile fire? I had much work to do to find out these answers. I know I will definitely call Dr. H.

CHAPTER 5

My leer jet lands at Melbourne International Airport at approximately 6:00 a.m. and taxies to a waiting limousine. I notice that there are several government customs agents waiting to inspect the plane and question us because of the high level of security that the world put in effect in the aftermath of what has happened.

The customs agents, satisfied with their search and their questions correctly answered, allow me and my staff members to depart. The limousine takes us to StereoOpticon. I tell Ms. Waters to schedule a staff meeting for late this afternoon.

We all retreat to the suites to refresh and rest. I know that we still have so much work to do on the technical aspects of the recently installed upgrades. Even though testing was successful on all the new upgrades, the upgrades must maintain a constant link to the satellites and the computers on board the satellites.

I retreat to my penthouse apartment. I look out of the window at the spectacular view below. I see a pod of dolphins breaking the surface of the Tasman Sea and then disappear slightly under the ocean only to reappear again and again as they make their way out to the open sea. This scene of serenity is quickly erased when the chaotic scenes from the news intrude on my mind.

I am absolutely dumbfounded by what I see and hear. I am

glued to the television despite a deep feeling of fatigue. Helicopters have begun flights from Richmond, Virginia, which is on the edge of the devastation. The helicopters are trying to film the outer perimeter of the blast radius. Nuclear fallout makes visibility very difficult, and the fear of radiation poisoning makes it impossible to venture inside the blast radius.

Meteorological reports have confirmed that the wind direction at the time of the blast was northeast. However, most of the nuclear fallout has been blowing out toward the Atlantic Ocean. An arctic cold front blowing down from Canada has met a warmer front moving up from the south, and the two fronts have come together around Washington, DC. Maryland and Philadelphia may be effected by the nuclear fallout in the future, but reports are still being evaluated about the extent of the damage these areas will sustain.

International reports have also confirmed the detonation of a nuclear missile near Israel, but no specific information is available at the present time. Officials are positioning satellites over the region, but reports of wild sandstorms have made visibility impossible at the present. I listen to reports in rapture.

I am stunned back out of a surreal world at 12:30 p.m. by my preprogrammed stereo playing Johan Bach. I seem to drift momentarily in the wonderful music that transports me into a wakeful dream state. I stare ahead and see the television, and I am suddenly roused to full consciousness, realizing the vast devastation that has happened over the past several hours.

After I turn off the stereo, I increase the volume of the current news reports. Many are concerned about the status of the US representatives and the country's president.

There are some initial reports that President Gunman may have been killed in the nuclear blast. Reports are now saying that according to national security protocol, the president would have been taken to a hardened bunker below ground at Capitol Hill.

Further reports of the President's status can only be confirmed by the detection of an emergency beacon that is transmitted automatically from the bunker when the doors are sealed. No confirmation has been reported because of the electronic distortion caused by the nuclear blast. Military officials have confirmed that they have begun a rescue operation. They are using the most sophisticated machinery and equipment available to rescue the survivors and evacuate as many personnel as possible. The search and rescue operation has been dubbed *Operation Chief Extraction*. The military has promised continuous updates on the progress of this very difficult procedure.

The updates continue, but there's also a story on the Middle East. Ground zero of the second nuclear blast has not yet been confirmed near the city of Tel Aviv. The fallout from the blast has extended to Amman, Jordan, and the southern outskirts of Damascus, Syria. Sandstorms have continued in the region, and they are widespread throughout the area. This makes it hard to assess the actual damage. The radiation levels remain high in the region, preventing rescue operations and the delivery of much-needed medical supplies.

Winds have been reported to be swirling and blowing in a general southeast direction through Jordan into Saudi Arabia, spreading radiation and nuclear fallout.

It is unclear what the true impact of the blast will be on the future of those individuals downwind. Reports indicate massive evacuations of those people in the path of the radiation. In an unprecedented show of compassion, all of the neighboring countries have opened their borders to the refugees, and they are trying to supply as much food and water and medical supplies as possible.

The whole region remains unstable despite the government officials' compassion in dealing with the regional catastrophe.

I grab my laptop and switch it on to check the satellite communications networks. Despite the ground interruptions to communications because of the high level of nuclear fallout, which is currently unavoidable, the networks are operating within normal standards. Signals between the four operating satellites orbiting around the Earth are functioning properly. I then checks my emergency call center to find out if I missed any calls. I listen to a message from the Russian president telling us to respond because this incident is a serious matter of national security.

I immediately call President Volochek and schedule a secure conference Internet meeting between him, Mr. Ballarat, and Ms. Cordero to address the issues with the Russian communications. I assure the Russian president that all issues will be resolved promptly and that there is no need for him to be physically present at this time.

I then call my senior executive, Mr. Ballarat, and advise him that today's meetings will be canceled because of the tragedies that have unfolded. I also advise him that he has an early morning Skype session with the Russian president. I have the utmost confidence in Mr. Ballarat's abilities and in Ms. Cordero's fluent Russian. I advise him to keep all high-level executive personnel in their suites for the time being and maintain enough staff to perform necessary operations on the upgrades.

I then call Ms. Waters and advise her of the recent decisions I have made. I tell her to make sure my requests are implemented.

I switch off my laptop and retreat to my small kitchen for a bite to eat. I retire to the bedroom to relax and watch more television for continuous updates on the worldwide situation, curious about how things will unfold. It seems as though I am compelled by a strange force as I gaze upon the large television.

I am startled out of a trance by the cell phone ringing. Mr. Ballarat is reporting that the company has received numerous calls by many different heads of state requesting the communications services for their governmental departments. I give the go-ahead to begin service to as many new customers as the system will support. With a tone of excitement in his voice, Mr. Ballarat acknowledges my reply. He then comments that the system has not even neared its maximum capacity yet because of the recent upgrades.

I confirm this fact and reply, "Organize all the department heads for late afternoon meetings tomorrow to discuss the new objectives the company will need in order to bring aboard the new clients."

Mr. Ballarat responds, "Yes, sir."

I return to the mesmerizing reports on the news channel. It is dawn on the East Coast of the United States, and reports are still flowing in from all correspondence outside of Washington, Baltimore, and Philadelphia.

Government agencies in all these areas are reporting that they are trying to establish communications. The fallout from the blast has slowly begun to blow out to the Atlantic Ocean, although radiation levels remain extremely high. Military vehicles equipped to stand the effects of radiation are heading to the Capitol Building in Washington, DC.

There is a mass evacuation in progress from the Philadelphia and New York City areas. Helicopters have shown scenes of violence, looting, and mass chaos throughout Philadelphia and New York City.

The reports also show a change in the wind direction. The National Weather Service has reported winds coming from the south have added to the mass exodus. All roads leading out of the two cities are congested and overloaded, making movement very slow and very perilous.

Police and fire services are stretched to the limit and are working around the clock, putting out fires and trying to control the numerous looters and those pillaging businesses and homes.

A state of emergency has been declared along the northeast coast, and martial law has been declared. The military has already been mobilized and has issued a warning to all civilians to cease and desist all illegal activities. Those who disregard these warnings will be apprehended or shot on sight.

There have been reports from military officials that the President has the capability to communicate through the use of a satellite telephone. Military officials also report that the hardened facilities are vacuum sealed and equipped with food, water, oxygen, and antiradiation suits necessary for their extraction.

The latest report from military officials have the rescue vehicles entering the greater Washington, DC, area. They are about five kilometers from the extraction point. Debris is everywhere, making progress slow, and the destruction of buildings and other structures makes navigation difficult.

These vehicles are equipped with remote television cameras. Officials have promised pictures of the area and the operation as soon as they can relay the data to a satellite and distribute it over the world. These images will be broadcast nationwide within the hour. Images of the rescue operation will follow, but no time frame has been set because of the unknown circumstances.

The focus then shifts back to the Middle East. Visibility in most areas is extremely difficult. Weather reports indicate that the sandstorms will subside in the near future. Analysts believe that Israeli bunkers are the best engineered and equipped, making survival likely. Government officials in these affected countries have yet to comment on the number of people the bunkers can hold or the time frame that the bunkers can support life. Reliable information is difficult to obtain at the moment in the Middle East.

However, communications are beginning to trickle in that the missile detonation occurred in the Mediterranean Sea. Millions of lives have been saved either by the Patriot Missile System knocking the missile off course or by divine intervention. Either way, a catastrophic event has been avoided.

I am deep in thought, taking in everything. I begin to construct my own ideas on how to improve the current situation. I wonder how much money and leadership will be necessary to make the world a stable place to live in, one where every inhabitant can live his or her life without the fear of being vaporized in a split second.

My attention wanders back to a CNN exclusive report that shows the extraction team at the site of the underground bunker at Capitol Hill. People get to see the first images from the blast now. The extraction crew has begun to clear debris from around the bunker in order to recover President Gunman. The military sets up additional vehicles in order to decontaminate the survivors. There is also a search and rescue team on a mission to find any survivors outside of the bunkers. The scene around Capitol Hill looks grim.

There are no reports of any survivors from Capitol Hill yet. The top dome of the Capitol Building was completely blown off by the blast. Very few of the Greek-style support beams remain standing.

On a more positive note, most of the debris is scattered away from the building. This will make the rescue operations easier. CNN continues to televise live scenes of operation chief extraction. At the same time, analysts continue to deliver reports as they come in. Analysts believe that the outlook for the federal representatives who were on Capitol Hill at the time of the blast looks grim. Most of the federal agencies have ceased operating. The entire federal government has been effectively shut down.

Every state in the union has declared a state of emergency, and all the borders of the United States have been closed. This means that travel in and out of the country has been suspended. Some states have even closed their own borders.

State highway patrolman are not allowing people to cross state lines in certain areas. However, evacuations are continuing in the Philadelphia, New York City, and the Boston area because of the fear of radiation poisoning if the winds change to a northerly direction. The latest report from the National Weather Service shows that winds are now moving in a northerly direction. The traffic congestion stretches from New York City to as far north as Manchester, Vermont.

The National Guard in conjunction with the state highway patrolmen have closed off all traffic trying to head south toward Washington, DC. They have opened the southerly direction lanes for people heading north in order to ease the traffic congestion. This stretch of traffic extends bumper to bumper out to the outskirts of Albany, New York, 150 miles north of New York City.

Traffic is being diverted to the north of Albany and to the west of Albany toward Buffalo. The state highway has also closed any eastward lanes. Authorities will eventually utilize these lanes for the traffic flow to move west, essentially allowing traffic to only move in one direction.

The national emergency broadcast system has been advising motorists to move south or west of the blast area. Unfortunately, panic has set in, and the highways are overcongested with motorists. The National Guard and highway patrol are trying to persuade motorists to exit immediately and proceed in a westerly direction. "Progress is slow because of the heavy traffic," the news anchor says in a somber voice.

Nearly twenty-four hours after the president was forced to take refuge in the bunker at Capitol Hill, pictures now show men beginning to exit the rubble. Several men assist and surround one man, who seems to be wearing the presidential seal on his antiradiation suit. As the men move closer to the decontamination vehicle, one man raises his hand and begins to wave. He then thrusts his fist into the air and shakes it vigorously in a show of triumph.

The whole crew at CNN begins to cheer, and the anchors clap as they realize the president has just been rescued. There are only four men other than the president who have been rescued. However, this is an uplifting scene amongst the devastation. The president enters the decontamination vehicle and waves one last time. One by one, the rest of the survivors enter the decontamination vehicle. *Operation Chief Extraction* is a glowing success story amidst the devastation and destruction of just twenty hours earlier.

The scene now shifts focus to another evacuation crew stationed in front of the White House. Reports indicate that the first lady and VP Sands took refuge in a bunker underneath the White House. The pictures from the military rescue crew cameras show that the White House has suffered massive damage. The mood of the broadcast has changed from jubilant to very somber in a matter of moments.

CHAPTER 6

Pat and I are now safely in the alternate operations headquarters at the Cheyenne Mountain Complex located in Colorado Springs. I am now in my office many stories below the surface in another bunker. I see Pat walk in, and I gesture for him to take a seat.

I begin, "Pat, the United States has just suffered its worst disaster in history. We must investigate this attack vigorously. It is of the utmost importance that we identify those responsible. It is just as important that we identify how this attack was accomplished. I want everyone to have at their disposal all the means necessary to investigate the entire series of events leading up to the launch and detonation of the nuclear missiles. This investigation must become our highest priority until further notice. Pat, I would like you to organize teams to begin the intensive investigative procedures. I would also like you to appoint a team to investigate our current launch capabilities.

"Next on the agenda is the fact that we must hold emergency elections in order to reinstate the federal government. As of 9:00 a.m. on this day by presidential order number 10070, I declare that emergency election procedures begin at once in every state of the union. This will be a massive undertaking, and if additional staff are needed, the approval is hereby given.

"I will speak to the American people this evening on every major network. Our communications network has performed brilliantly at every step after the disaster. I must instill confidence in them that the federal government will continue to operate. I will need the initial procedures necessary to start emergency elections. I will inform the American people of the process. I want constant updates on the rescue and evacuation of any survivors from the attack."

Pat says, "All right, I will get on that after we are done here. I would like to give you the current situation on the extraction efforts of Carol and VP Sands. The extraction crew is taking longer than expected. There was an accident. Carol has a concussion. She's all right. She's awake. The rescuers are taking all the necessary precautions. As soon as word comes through, I will immediately inform you."

"Thank you, Pat. That means a lot to me. I would like to talk to her as soon as possible. I know there are many people who have suffered great loss because of this horrible and cowardly act.

"Zac, I know we all will make time to mourn the loss of our friends and loved ones and our countrymen. I don't want to seem callous; however, I must change the subject and talk to you about the pressing needs of the country. I have the short list you requested for the new cabinet members in order for the executive office to operate to its fullest capabilities," Pat says in a solemn tone. "I have done my best to select the most qualified individuals to fill all the vacancies."

"Thank you, Pat. You know me and what I expect better than anyone, and I trust your judgment. Let's invite everyone on the list here so we can speak to them. We are in unprecedented circumstances, and we must act quickly and wisely," I say.

"Yes, sir." He then continues, "Zac, I have great news for you. The second missile reached its maximum range and went down in the Mediterranean Sea. There was no land explosion. I have been on the phone with Ambassador Snow from Israel, and he assures me that everyone in the region is safe. The heads of state are waiting for the sandstorms to subside. They will make a statement in the near future."

I respond, "That is great news, Pat. Now if you will excuse me, I have a speech to write."

"Thank you, Mr. President." Pat gets up and exits then.

Before I can begin writing the speech, an overwhelming feeling of pain hits me. Tears begin to roll down my cheeks. I don't fight them. I just let them flow freely. No speech writer in the world can say what has to be said. This is a speech only the president of the United States can write. I must inform the American people of what is happening. I must put to rest the spread of panic. I must offer hope and stability. I must undo the terror that has been done.

On my first full day in Colorado Springs, I conduct meetings, provide leadership where none previously existed, talk on the phone to several leaders from around the world, and write a compelling speech, and now I will deliver the speech to the American people.

I begin at precisely 8:30 p.m. eastern standard time. "Good evening, my fellow Americans. Would everyone please join me in a moment of silence to honor those who have perished during the nuclear disaster.

"Thank you. I would like to talk to you tonight about the unprovoked attacks on Washington, DC, and Israel. Two nuclear missiles were launched from Minot, North Dakota. One was detonated over Washington, DC, and one near Israel. The launch of these missiles was not authorized by myself or anyone else within the government of the United States.

"We have begun an intensive investigation into the unauthorized detonation of these missiles. I would like to extend my most sincere condolences to those who have lost their lives in this country and in Israel. We are currently taking steps to rescue and evacuate those individuals who have survived this horrific attack. We will also extend any help that the Israeli government may need in order to help them as well.

"Today I have issued Executive Order 10070, which will put into effect emergency elections in order to reinstate the legislative branch of the federal government. These emergency elections will take place within the next thirty days. State governmental agencies will begin accepting nominations immediately. There will be a brief time period for those nominees to campaign for seats on the federal government.

"I have also issued Executive Order 10071. This order will change the nation's capital from Washington, DC, to Kansas City, Missouri. I chose Kansas City because of its central location within the United States. New construction will begin in order to house the Congress of the United States. The legislative branch of the American government will rise once again and fulfill its functions.

"In order to carry out the guidelines of the twenty-fifth amendment to the Constitution of the United States, it will be necessary to have a legislative branch actively sitting. It is of the utmost importance that we do not lose sight of the intentions of our forefathers, especially now, in the hour of our need. We cannot deviate our Constitution.

"We would like to imagine a world without terrorism, a world where no one fears the paths they walk. There is no worthwhile belief that combines the thought of violence with the act of violence. Any such acts in order to achieve a political purpose must be condemned. It has now become an even greater priority of the United States to actively seek out these individuals or groups of individuals who actively participate in such acts. The United States will now take all steps necessary in order to eradicate this threat to mankind as a whole.

"However, in the immediate future, we as Americans have much to do. I have recalled a large portion of our military forces back to the United States from overseas. They will assist in restoring peace on the East Coast. It will also be necessary to utilize the armed forces to ensure the national security of the United States.

"A perimeter has been established around the blast zone. No one will be allowed inside this parameter. Areas outside of the perimeter have been deemed safe. I assure the American people that it is now safe to return to your homes. There is no further threat of nuclear war. Everything is being done to ensure your safety.

"It is in this time of great pain and sorrow that we must rise above these feelings and act in the best interests of our countrymen and our country. It is a time for healing, not panic. It is a time to rebuild and not destroy. It is a time to grow as individuals and as a country. Please work with me in order that we may achieve these goals. Our forefathers would have wanted us to rise up to the great challenges that we face now and in the future. Everyone must now help one another in order for our country to prosper. I pledge to keep the American people safe from harm and to rebuild America. God bless you all, and God bless America."

I sign off with a heavy heart. I know the speech was brief, but one message at time. I just hope I got my message across. Pat follows me to my office.

He shuts the door and says, "Zac, I have dispatched a team to investigate the circumstances around the launches at Minot. I will keep you up to date as reports come in. We have organized a team to work in conjunction with state governments to initiate federal elections.

"The orders to recall our overseas troops are being completed. They will begin to trickle home effective immediately.

"I have organized a team to begin new construction in

Kansas City to house the legislative and the judiciary branches of government. Construction has begun on the new Capitol Building.

"Currently, there are no reports of any survivors from Capitol Hill. We do have decontamination crews searching Washington, DC, for any survivors. Search and rescue efforts are still underway at the White House as well."

"Excellent work, Pat. What is the situation in Philadelphia and New York City and in the surrounding areas? I would like to stay current on the overall situation in these areas. I want to keep the American people updated as often as possible," I say.

Pat responds in pure military fashion, "Yes, sir. With the addition of the National Guard and the military reservists, we are beginning to put a stop to the looting. The highways are beginning to operate as normal, and the panic seems to be dying down. But I will keep you updated on all the situations as information comes in. I have the intelligence community stretched to their limits."

"Thanks, Pat. I knew I could count on you, and Pat, keep stretching the intelligence community."

Pat smiles just a little and then says, "Thank you, Mr. President."

Pat turns and leaves the office. He seems to know when I want to be left alone. But I thank the heavens above that I have Pat as my right-hand man. I really don't know what I would do without him. If there was ever a model of friendship, loyalty, and brains, it would be him.

CHAPTER 7

I am sitting with Mr. Ballarat and Ms. Cordero. We are about to contact President Volochek.

I say, "Put the call through, Stewart."

He responds, "Right now."

As Stewart brings the president online for a video conference call, I inform him that I will talk initially. Then I will hand over the specifics and the linguistics to the two of them. They both nod their heads in agreement. I move in front of the large computer monitor, waiting for the president's face to appear.

When I see the president, I begin, "Mr. President, it's good to see you, and thank you for taking our call. We are on a secure line on my end."

"Thank you, Harry. I have a secure line as well. I must ask you these questions. I'm sure you understand with the state of the world such as it is."

"Of course, Mr. President," I say. "Ask me whatever you like. I have Mr. Ballarat and Ms. Cordero here with me. I'm sure you know Ms. Cordero. Mr. Ballarat is my finest executive. He knows the company's hardware inside and out. He is going to be handling any issues that may arise for the foreseeable future. If you are unhappy with any results or have any concerns whatsoever, you can contact me at any time."

"Thank you, I will. I do have some serious issues to bring up that need your immediate attention. Do you understand me?"

"I do, Mr. President."

President Volochek begins, "During the US launch of the rogue missiles, I, of course, was in my bunkered command center, and during this time I made the order to launch one nuclear missile and target Washington, DC. My system failed to respond to that order. Do I make myself clear, sir?"

"You do, and I will have Mr. Ballarat do diagnostics to find out if there was a glitch in the communications system that may have blocked your commands. I know this may get a little technical, so Ms. Cordero is standing by to interpret and work with your technicians to resolve this issue. I agree that it is unacceptable not to have control of your arsenal. We will get to the bottom of this, Mr. President. If we can't solve your problems, we will reinstate all your original software at no cost," I conclude.

The look on the president's face began to change from stoic to hostile. "Damn you. I know the communications upgrades had something to do with the lack of response of my orders to launch. Don't play games with me!"

"Mr. President, I will never play games with you, especially when it comes to matters of national security. I have been integrating the system with the satellites myself. Mr. President, I assure you that as far as I can tell from the work I have done myself on integrating the whole communications system for the entire world, there are no visible problems. However, this does not mean that there may be some problems throughout the system that cause interruptions. Mr. Ballarat will see to it that there are no more interruptions in your system. I guarantee it. You have my word, Mr. President."

"Dr. Hornswoggle, how do you explain the loss of our capability to launch a nuclear weapon shortly after your upgrades were installed?" the president says calmly but firmly.

"I have no explanation at this time, Mr. President. However, I would like to be given the opportunity to find out ... if you will let me."

"I would appreciate that, but I will run my own diagnostics in conjunction with yours," the president says in perfect English.

"We will begin immediately, Mr. President," I say.

"I look forward to seeing the results of your diagnostics." The president has a serious look on his face.

"Absolutely, Mr. President. I will now turn everything over to Mr. Ballarat and Ms. Cordero. Good day, Mr. President."

"Good day to you, Doctor. And I, too, know everything will be resolved to my satisfaction," President Volochek says.

I get up to leave and give Stuart and Ms. Cordero a confident nod, instilling more confidence, I hope. I have to have faith in my staff. But I know that this is ultimately my responsibility. I am confident that my company can improve the lives of people around the world. I now have a vast amount of wealth. As of today, I am the wealthiest man on the planet. My wealth will double in the next six months. My priorities have now shifted. Men of great wealth sometimes seek to become humanitarians. I will take this effort a step further. I will become the man who unites this planet for the first time. I will become the leader that this world needs now. Especially now.

CHAPTER 8

As dawn rises in Colorado Springs, I also rise. Deep purple increasingly overtakes the black horizon. Yellow streaks begin to illuminate the mountain ranges. The thought of the sunrise is enough for me to rise and face another difficult day. I can't see the morning blaze, but I know it's there. Each day I wake up without my wife. Instead I wake up in this hellhole. I wake up and imagine a sunrise for me and everyone else on this planet. It's another day closer to finding out who did this to my country. That is what is on my mind when I wake up. Finding out who did this to us and bringing them to justice. I know I have the world to consider and the safety of everyone in it, but I also know I have a responsibility to be ruthless in the hunt and maybe even kill everyone involved in the attack against the United States.

However, I keep these thoughts to myself.

I am very anxious to meet with Pat to get his updates and begin the meetings scheduled for the day. There are many important positions to fill in this cabinet and the federal government. But most importantly, I want the updates on the missile launches and the investigation.

I know the individuals who were invited to meet with me are beginning to descend deep below the surface of the earth to the main operations center. There is also a new influx of military and civilian personnel who must fill vacant positions in order to run the main operations center.

I can hear Pat' s voice spouting orders. I know we are in good hands with him running the staff. I can predict that tension will be high as 9:00 a.m. quickly approaches. I can hear loud voices throughout the office area. Regardless of the level of anxiety, I know quality work is being completed. Organization is beginning to take shape. All who have been called by their country will undoubtedly display true professionalism.

I enter the briefing room off to the side of the main operations floor. All the attendees are present—Pat, the joint chief of staff, Admiral Sheridan, and a few staff members. Everyone greets me by saying, "Good morning, Mr. President." The top secret meeting is immediately underway.

Pat stands and begins the briefing. "Mr. President, ladies and gentlemen, this briefing is classified top secret, no foreigners allowed, SCI level 5 and above only. I'm familiar with everyone here, but if anyone needs their clearance updated, please see me after the briefing. This briefing is a current intelligence briefing on the last twenty-four hours. I have organized the investigative team on the missile launches. The lead team is comprised of Special Agents Blanchard and Davis. They are the finest men the CIA has to offer. They have begun the initial inquiry into the nuclear accident to establish the truth behind the incident. I have also dispatched key teams who are at this moment analyzing the computer systems and programs at the launch site.

"I have dispatched all local CIA squads and computer specialists to attain vital intelligence information. They will analyze the launch and the flight path of each missile and how they were guided to their targets. It is extremely important to determine how the missiles were guided. This will lead us closer to whomever was behind the incident. Everyone is currently under suspicion and being investigated."

I interrupt Pat and say, "We know some type of sabotage or influence on the launch occurred. I didn't launch. It is of extreme importance to find out how this was achieved and prevent this from ever happening again. For the moment, we cannot prevent this from happening again. I'm going to order all nuclear missile sites within the United States shut down. I'm going to recall all nuclear submarines back to port to undergo analysis and maintenance.

"At the moment, we are our own worst enemy. These operations must remain highly secret. There must be no leaks of the military movements back to our shores. I want to reroute all the nuclear submarines using frequent directional changes to try to disguise the movements for as long as possible.

"I can see the looks of concern on all your faces. I assure you this is the best course of action for the immediate future. I have told no one of these plans. It may be a leap of faith, but whoever is doing this must have the ability to stop a launch as well as execute a launch. This may allow us a window of opportunity to complete necessary investigations."

Pat continues, "Yes, Mr. President. Is there anything else that needs immediate attention?"

"Yes, Pat, I understand we have not been able to determine the whereabouts of the ex-CIA director Nichols. I would like you to investigate if there is any possibility that he would have anything to do with the launch of the missiles. I understand things are very chaotic at the moment. I also understand this is a scenario that is unimaginable. However, it is one avenue that we must take during our investigations. All right, I think we have our work cut out for us for the next twenty-four hours. Everyone meet here tomorrow, same time."

I stand and start to head to my office, but I talk to Pat on the way. "Pat, let's have all the civilian personnel who are up for cabinet positions meet with you first. This is your staff too, and I trust your judgement. I have some very detailed work I need to get done today."

"You got it, Zac," Pat says, and then he hurries off. I go into my office to begin my plan off attack to rid the world of the most dangerous terrorist the world has ever known.

***

I leave Zac and realize the huge amount of responsibility he has entrusted upon me. I have a mountain of work to do, but that doesn't faze me in the least. I relish the opportunity to serve my country to the best of my abilities. I won't let Zac or my country down.

I immediately track down the generals necessary to execute the president's orders pertaining to the military. I then advise all the distinguished civilian personnel that they must meet with me in the main briefing room.

There isn't a second to waste, and all the information I gain is critical. Reports from various governmental departments are beginning to appear on my desk. But most are from Langley. The CIA headquarters keeps me current on their updates of the multiple situations.

Never before has United States been so vulnerable to complete annihilation by its enemies without the ability to respond. At no time in history has the entire world been so unstable and unsafe for everyone.

The minutes fly by, and I head to the main briefing room for the next round of important meetings. I begin, "Good morning, everyone, and thank you for coming. I know this is an unconventional meeting. I would like to speak to everyone at the same time. This will save us time, and it will be a chance for everyone to get to know one another. You have all been chosen because of your outstanding contributions to the United States and your outstanding reputations. I feel confident that everyone in this room is qualified to hold the positions they've been chosen for.

"Everyone will hold positions within the president's cabinet. It is only a matter of determining who will hold what specific positions within the cabinet. Everyone will have to live on site for an undetermined amount of time. There are some requirements that may not suit every individual. If anyone has a problem with these requirements, they will have to be dismissed."

As the interview process nears its end, not one individual has decided to decline the sacrifices necessary in order to serve the president. During the whole process, I take notes. I am confident that everyone present will be an integral member of the president's cabinet.

Then I bring the meeting to a close, and I conclude, "The president will make the official and formal offer of positions tomorrow. I would like to thank everyone for stepping up to serve the United States of America. There are living quarters waiting for each of you. If you go see the president's secretary, she will have your assignments. I will see each of you tomorrow. I look forward to working with all of you. Our work together won't be easy. However, your service to the president and our country comes at a time of its greatest need."

I escort everyone out of the briefing room and direct them to where they will be assigned living quarters. I go to my office and go over my notes and match names to fill vacancies within the cabinet. I make careful decisions and weigh all the qualifications necessary.

They must be leaders and followers if they are to succeed and must follow the command of their president. They must be individual thinkers when time is pressing. They must work as a team because we will only be able to rebuild the United States through teamwork.

The morning seems to fly by. It is almost noon. I decide to check on Zac and see if he wants company for lunch. My next meeting after lunch is with Special Agents Blanchard and Davis of the CIA. These men are the pride of our country when it comes to solving criminal investigations.

I knock on Zac's door and enter. He invites me in, and I take a seat. I begin telling the president that Special Agents Blanchard and Davis are the two best investigators in the United States. I inform the president that they have solved every case they have ever worked on to everyone's satisfaction. Blanchard and Davis were out of the country at the time of the blast. I immediately recalled them from overseas. If these two men can't solve this mystery, no one can.

I also inform the president that new elections are being organized across the country. Candidates have already come forward in almost every state. The election process is proceeding as planned.

I inform the presiden of another piece of uplifting news. Senator Brazil from Vermont was not present in Washington, DC, at the time of the bombing. He was in Vermont because his wife was giving birth to their first child. Two individuals from the House of Representatives were also absent—one from California and one from Texas.

I then change the subject to the national security of the United States. I explain to the president that technicians and investigators are still working on how the missiles were launched. As of noon today, there is no capability to launch any nuclear weapons. All the weapons have been taken off-line until further notice. Everyone is working around the clock to come up with any evidence or answers about who manipulated the launches.

I also update the president on the mass evacuations that have occurred in the Northeast. Most of the people have returned to their homes. National Guard units and police have controlled the rioting and looting. Normalcy is beginning to take shape in the major cities along the Northeast border.

I also inform the president that search and rescue teams are working diligently in Washington, DC, to find any survivors. They have found thousands wounded and have relocated them to hospitals. They will continue their operations within the DC area until they are satisfied that everyone has been found and removed from the area.

I tell the president that Carol is still in the hospital undergoing tests. She has been put in a comatose state because she has a hemorrhage in her brain. VP Sands was released this morning, and he is on his way to a separate location at Peterson Air Force Base.

I am happy to inform the president that the nuclear cloud over Washington, DC, has moved out over the Atlantic Ocean and is beginning to dissipate. The severe wind and sandstorms in and around Israel have ended. There are no reports of any casualties from that region.

***

At precisely 1:00 p.m., Pat leads Special Agents Blanchard and Davis into my office. I am struck by their appearance. They both look incredibly young for their ages. I shake each man's hand before we sit down.

I begin, "Gentleman, I appreciate the both of you getting here so quickly. I'm sure Pat has filled you in on most of the details and your objectives."

Both men nod in agreement.

"Good. I can't stress the importance of this investigation. It is vital. Time is of the essence, and there can be no rest until the both of you have found who is responsible. I want the person or persons responsible for this atrocity. Gather as much evidence as possible in order to convict in an international court of law.

"I need you. More importantly, your country needs you, and the rest of the world is relying on you. I will be looking forward to hearing updates twice a day on your progress. The both of you have all the support necessary at your disposal. Are there any questions?"

Both men respond in unison, "No, Mr. President."

"All right then. Godspeed in your endeavors," I say.

Both men chime in, "Thank you, Mr. President."

Agent Blanchard says, "We will work nonstop on this investigation to find who is responsible. Count on us."

As they walk toward the door, I say, "I am counting on the both of you, and so is your country."

Pat exits with both agents, and I am left alone in my office. The news of the day had some uplifting points, but I can't help worrying about Carol. I can't keep calling the doctor for updates. I just have to have faith in their expertise. I have to have faith in everyone's abilities to do their jobs as best as they can without micromanaging.

CHAPTER 9

I am very excited about this evening because I am about to address the world. I have been preparing several speeches to deliver. These speeches will lay the foundation of my views on world politics. I have time booked on radio stations around the world. I will also appear on a website I recently unveiled.

I walk into the boardroom, where technical crews have set up their equipment. Cameras are set up and tested. Microphones are positioned and tested. I have a makeup crew working diligently to perfect my appearance.

I am about to embark on a great and demanding challenge. I may be an unknown commodity at the moment, but this will change. I take a seat and clear my throat, ready to begin.

The director of media chimes in, "You're live in five, four, three—" Two seconds later he points to me.

"People throughout the world, let me introduce myself," I say. "My name is Dr. Horatio Hornswoggle. I am the President and CEO of StereoOpticon. My company is the leading worldwide provider of communications. I am able to speak to you today through my own satellite network. I have also sent a signal around the world via the radio. I have a sincere hope that my message seeks out as many people around the world as possible.

"I would like to start off by telling everyone listening a little bit about myself. I have been very fortunate in my lifetime. I have obtained a doctorate degree in economics as well as computer technology and communications. I have been very successful in the business world as well. I have been chief executive officer of several companies in which I have a controlling interest. These companies range from state-of-the-art computer development and enhancement to cutting-edge communications systems through my satellite operations.

"I feel with the recent events that have developed around the world, there is a need for an individual to try to make a positive impact in our world today, to reinstill confidence in all human beings so that our world can move forward from this horrible tragedy that has struck so many great and important people.

"I know I have something to offer every single person around the world. Together, we can work to rebuild confidence in the human race despite the evils and atrocities that have been committed by mankind. We all must look to the future and make it a bright one for us and our children. It is this rebuilding of all lives around the world that I speak of today.

"There exists a very unstable political environment in many countries around the world. I have doubts that these countries will be able to mend and restore their past political stability. There is a need for a greater force to work in conjunction with all political systems around the globe.

"What I propose to all countries around the globe as well as all individuals is a simple challenge. That challenge is accountability by all people and governments in the world. It may sound like a simple goal, but I ask everyone to ponder this statement for a moment. It may be achieved if everyone cooperates and puts forth an effort like the human race has never seen in its history.

"I have stepped to the forefront today to develop this idea and make it a reality. I will make my ideas and my actions available in order to make this dream a reality for all people on earth. I will develop this idea of global accountability further.

"This may seem like a monumental task, but I assure you it is attainable by all of us. The world is in need of one body that transcends the virtually ineffective United Nations. They have failed to deal with rogue countries or groups of evil people who are not being held accountable for their actions.

"There is a need for a body of individuals who represents the world as a whole—one that can deal with the unique problems that the future holds. Together, we can develop this complex body to bring about a future where people can have peace of mind wherever they live.

"It is a responsibility that we all have. I will explain what is necessary for this to happen in more detail in my next speech. This speech will be a live broadcast from Mount Olympus in Greece. Many of the world's media representatives will be given a paid invitation to this next speech. Anyone who receives one of the special invitations must make the utmost effort to attend. Great expense has gone into preparation for this next event.

"I would ask the media representatives to have a least one question prepared for me to answer. My answers will come in the form of yes or no only because there are a great many of you. My responses may lead to more questions. I do not want any misconceptions about the tasks we are about to undergo.

"This speech is scheduled in three days from today. I will leave you all now, and hope that I've instilled in you some faith and inspiration. Some men say that space is the final frontier. Well, I say that bringing the world together on a global level is the new frontier that mankind must develop and participate in. Thank you for your attention, and good-bye to everyone for now."

All of my staff are present, listening to the speech. They wear looks of amazement and confusion on their faces. I get up and confront the staff. I explain to them what I am about to attempt. I express my confidence in their abilities to perform their duties in my absence. Content that the staff understands what is happening, I excuse myself for the evening.

I go to the suite to relax. I need to watch as many news reports on the current situation as possible before sleep overtakes me. This will provide needed insight. I know that the global government needs resolve many issues.

CHAPTER 10

Forty-eight hours have passed. I am amazed that Agent Blanchard and Davis are back in that short amount of time. I knew they were making progress from their updates, but this is too good to be true. I'm skeptical at this point, but hopeful.

I enter the main briefing room. Everyone stands. They say, "Good afternoon, Mr. President."

I nod, and everyone sits. Present in the room is the commander of the joint chiefs of the US Armed Forces, Commander Sheridan. The new CIA director, William Ryan, Pat, and Agents Blanchard and Davis are also there.

Agent Blanchard leads the briefing off by stating, "Mr. President, we have narrowed the most probable suspects down to one probable person or entity and two possible governments. We feel at this time that we can't completely rule out the governments of China and North Korea with the evidence that has been uncovered. These two governments are notorious, as you well know, of hacking into computer systems.

"However, we feel that our prime suspect at this time is Dr. Hornswoggle, or as we have called him, *Dr. H*, and his company, StereoOpticon. He is the head of the most powerful communications company in the world. He has four satellites orbiting the Earth at high altitude. He has advanced degrees in computer technology. There is no one like him on the planet.

"He holds government contracts with the United States, as you know, the Russians, and the Chinese. Almost overnight he has quickly become the wealthiest man on the earth."

I have to interrupt at this point and ask Agent Blanchard, "How could a company that provides communication software to the Russians and the Chinese have clearance to contract with the US government as well? I thought he was vetted by the CIA and the National Security Council."

Agent Blanchard continues, "Mr. President, we asked the same question. We looked into that. The CIA has no record of ever investigating him. The NCS did investigate his company. They viewed his company as a state-of-the-art communications company. The US coms systems are aging rapidly. All the systems were in need of an upgrade. The National Security Council decided that it was worth the risk to obtain these vital upgrades. They didn't view him or his company as a threat."

I know everything that Agent Blanchard has told me is true. I take a deep breath before I ask my next question, but I have to ask. "Gentlemen, I must ask this question. Is there any evidence whatsoever that these incidents were caused by intelligence not of this world?"

I see Agent Blanchard and Davis look at each. Blanchard responds, "If you mean extraterrestrials, we have no evidence at this time to suggest the attacks were caused by anyone other than people from this world. Granted, if you use the logic of eliminating everything that is impossible and whatever is left, no matter how unlikely, is the truth, it might lead you down that path. We haven't discovered how this was done yet. But we are not going down that path just yet. We have considered it.

"There was an incident in the 1950s when the launch computers were shut down for a period of time. There was evidence of a high-frequency electronic pulse. The origin was unknown, and any further attempts to break down the signal failed. Whether this same pulse could activate the launch mechanism for the missiles is unknown. It does remain a possibility, and we must remain open to this fact. There were rumors of extraterrestrial sightings near the complex in Wyoming at the time of the shutdown. These rumors were dismissed without further evidence. This time nothing can be dismissed unless evidence absolutely suggests otherwise.

"However, we do think the technology used is of this planet. Mr. President, have you ever heard of quantum computers?"

I answer, "Of course, but that technology is still in its infancy."

Blanchard continues, "Mr. President, at this point it is the only plausible explanation. The United States has a working prototype. But it has many limitations. We assumed incorrectly that we were ahead of everyone else in its development."

I ponder all the information. "All right, thank you, gentlemen. I believe there is more work to be done to unravel this mystery. I will expect an update as soon as possible. You may go now."

Both men get up to leave and say, "Thank you, Mr. President."

I glanced over at the director of the CIA, William Ryan. I say, "Director, the CIA didn't even interview this man or check his background?"

I think he knew this was coming. He says, "Mr. President, I promise I will look into this. I can assure you that in the future this will never happen again."

I respond, "Director Ryan, I know you weren't in charge. I'm not holding you responsible. But yes, do look into it, and change that policy. No one gets through the cracks any longer."

"Yes, Mr. President," he says.

"All right, moving on. What intelligence do we have on the current nuclear capabilities of the Russians and the Chinese?"

Director Ryan says, "We have detected no launch signals from our satellites or our computer systems. This includes any test launches that may have been attempted without nuclear warheads. Our analysts believe that the Russians would have attempted to launch a nuclear missile while tracking the rogue inbound over Russian airspace.

"We must make the conclusion that they have no nuclear launch capability at this time. It is a dangerous conclusion, but until there is a test launch of one of their nuclear missiles, this is the position that the intelligence analysts have taken. As soon as there is evidence to the contrary, we will inform you immediately."

"All right, Director," I say. "We will assume you are correct for the time being. God help us if you're wrong."

I turn my attention to Admiral Sheridan and ask him, "Commander, what is the status of our nuclear submarines with regard to their launch capabilities and their repositioning en route to ports within the United States?"

Commander Sheridan responds, "All the nuclear submarines have no launch capability at this time. They are en route to ports spread out along the Atlantic and Pacific coastlines. It is our hope this will confuse anyone who might be tracking them. Mr. President, we have tried to test-launch several of our missiles without arming the nuclear warhead. All attempts to launch have failed thus far."

"Commander, stop any test launches. I want you to take all of the nuclear missiles off-line and shut down the command and control computers until further notice. Continue with your current course of action and bring our boys back safely," I say.

"Yes, sir, Mr. President," the commander says without hesitation.

"That will be all, Commander," I say.

"Thank you, Mr. President," the admiral says.

The only person now left in the room is Pat. I ask, "Have all the launch silos been taken off-line and effectively shut down across the United States?"

"They have, Zac," Pat answers.

"All right then, Pat, we don't have to worry about any more arbitrary launches of nuclear missiles for the time being, I hope. This puts us in a very vulnerable position for the moment. Maybe we're acting exactly as someone wants.

"I haven't been able to contact President Volochek yet. I'll keep trying.

"You understand now how important this investigation has become. Whoever is jamming our launch capabilities has just raised the stakes. This has now become our number-one priority, and we will not rest until we find out who is responsible and how they have achieved this feat."

Pat responds, "We're all on the same page now, Zac. I just hope God is on our page too."

"We may need God on our side for this one," I say.

I tell Pat that I need to be alone for my next duty. He bows his head and leaves. I take the list of missing persons who were members of the US government out of my desk. I can wait no more. The list is long, and the task is not an enviable one. I begin calling the family members, hoping to speak with them about their losses.

CHAPTER 11

Agents Blanchard and Davis have obtained the preliminary analysis of the signals that were used during the launch of the nuclear missiles. The men are alone in a briefing room at Peterson Air Force Base, where officials hand over the evidence.

Davis says, "The only evidence thus far are the unique signals that have been evaluated by the signal intelligence team. The signals reveal a very high-frequency electronic pulse. The origin was unknown, and all attempts to break down the signal have failed. No further evidence exists. Well, that doesn't leave us much to go on, does it?"

I respond, "Well, the pulse only lasted a very short time. That's something. I know nothing can be dismissed unless evidence absolutely suggests otherwise. But at this point, it is difficult to identify one man or one country behind the attacks. And the outrageous assumption of alien intervention is becoming more of a reality."

Davis looks at me and smiles. Then he says, "Our investigation is going to have to go to another level. I will call the company's headquarters and demand an interview with Dr. H. That means ignoring most of the rules about investigating. No throwing evidence at him. Not being able to surprise him, and worst of all, he's sure to have lawyers present to answer how they want him to."

I respond, "I'm not excited about the prospect of going undercover alone in a very dangerous operation. And it will take too long to infiltrate his company. Even then there are no guarantees we will find anything. I think the direct approach is best in this situation. What do you think?"

Davis thinks for several moments and then says, "We risk blowing the whole investigation that way. And what the hell do you know about quantum physics?"

"At the moment, about as much as you do."

Davis chuckles a little, shakes his head, and says, "You're taking lead investigator on this one, genius."

"Don't mind if I do, Watson. Don't worry so much. In eighteen years, have I ever let you down?"

"Well, no," Davis says begrudgingly.

"Okay then, what're we waiting for?" I say.

"You're gonna be the death of me. Y'all know that, right?" Davis says.

"Not while you're with me, brother. You're gonna have to do that alone."

"Yeah, you always say that. I'll make the call. Does it matter where we interview?"

I think for a moment, and then it hits me. "Yes, it does. Vegas!"

"Oh, boy. No, no, no, and no!"

"C'mon. It'll be fun. Trust me. There's a method to my madness," I say.

"You're gonna explain this method. But first, we need a crash course on quantum physics from the best. I'll make all the calls as usual. Where would you like to stay in Vegas, sir?" Davis says sarcastically.

"Well, Caesars Palace, of course, my dear Watson," I say.

"Of course," Davis responds.

This could be our finest hour or our worst nightmare. I know that this move may pose several risks. We won't tell anyone of our plans, not even the president. Davis doesn't know that yet, but he'll go along with it.

I know we have a few tricks up our sleeves to even the odds a bit. Failure is not an option.

CHAPTER 12

As the hundredth hour after the attack approaches, I prepare another small speech to give to the American people. I also know the world will be watching and listening. This hour will be a time to mourn all those who have lost their lives during this horrific attack.

I begin, "Good evening, my fellow Americans. As the hundredth hour after the attack on the United States nears, I feel it is necessary to address you again. I have just signed an executive order announcing a national day of mourning for all those who have lost their lives in the attack against America. This will be forever a national holiday—May 3, 2020. It is not one in which to celebrate and light fireworks but one when every man, woman, and child should bow their heads. They should bow their heads in respect of those who have perished in an attack against humanity as a whole. Flags around the country will fly at half-mast throughout the fifty states.

"I would like to apologize to everyone for a political stance that nuclear weapons are a means of defense. I would like to apologize for the corrupt logic that nuclear weapons deter violence between countries. I would like to apologize to the whole human race. Our violence has evolved to a point where the push of a button or the turn of the key could mean the end to humanity as we know it.

"I do vow to bring those responsible for these horrific acts to justice. I do not speak of retaliation toward those responsible, for to do so would be an act of vengeance—an act resulting in many more deaths of innocent people. To speak of an attack at this time would be most foolish. This is a day to mourn those who have lost their lives. It is a time to lessen the panic felt by millions of people in the United States as well as those around the world. It is a time to feel the loss of those we loved and honored and cherished in our lives. It is a time to mourn loss and begin the process of forgiving, but lest we forget what has happened and honor those lost. God bless you all. God bless those who've lost their lives, and most of all, God bless America."

CHAPTER 13

I am happy to see almost all of the journalists invited to Greece have attended. There is a huge crowd waiting. It is a gorgeous spring day. The sun is bright in a cloudless sky. The water is sky blue with white stars shooting along the crests of the waves. The sight is almost blinding it is so bright.

I wonder why so many people showed up. Probably out of curiosity. They wonder if this event will reveal the ravings of a lunatic or the birth of a genius.

I think they wonder if there is a remote possibility that one man could solve all the world's problems. They are intrigued, yet I think they are very skeptical.

I walk to the podium to the sound of very light applause. I begin, "Welcome, ladies and gentlemen from around the world. I am pleased to see that most of the invitations sent out have been accepted and that there's a wonderful turnout at today's speech. I would also like to welcome those people from around the world watching on television and on the Internet from their computers, laptops, and smart phones.

"Before I begin to take any questions, I would like to give everyone a brief outline of what I had promised in my first speech. I will begin with an overview of the global government.

"It will have three branches. The executive branch will be

headed by a president. There will be no vice president. The Senate and House of Representatives will make up the legislative and investigative body. The third branch of government will be the judicial branch, which will review all international law made by the legislative body.

"The whole process will be based on a democratic principle of government, but at the same time, it will be unique. It will not resemble any other form of the political system anywhere in the world. For example, the president of the global government will be elected by the Senate and the House of Representatives by a majority decision.

"The judicial branch of government will be comprised of eleven members. These eleven members will be chosen by the Senate through majority vote. They will review all laws passed and signed into law by the president.

"The Senate will have one representative from each country or ethnic group. Any laws passed in the House must also be voted on in the Senate and passed by a simple majority. Then the bill can be passed to the president. If the president signs off on the bill, it will become law. Unless, of course, the judiciary views it to be 'not in the best interest of the world as a whole.'

"There can be no laws made that deviate from these general principles.

"The House will be representative of each nation according to its population. Each ethnic or special interest group will be allowed one representative. The maximum number allowed for any one country is five representatives.

Once chosen, the president must be confirmed by the judicial branch. He may serve for only a three-year term and must stand down for three years after his term has ended. At this time the president may choose to head any committee of his or her choice within the House of Representatives. He or she may also sit as a member on two additional committees in the House or the Senate if the person so desires. However, the president may run for reelection again at a later date if the Senate and the House of Representatives nominate him as a candidate in a later election.

"Most importantly, while in office during his or her term as the president, if he or she is found to have acted in an unjust manner by the House and Senate after a special investigation has been conducted, a vote of no confidence may be initiated. Hearings will be conducted by the judiciary to determine if any unjust behavior is evident. If the judicial findings support the investigation of the House and Senate, then that President will be found unfit for office, and he or she will be removed. He or she will never be able to hold any position within the global government. Once removed, the president may be tried by the judiciary for the proper punishment.

"This is the beginning of the absolute accountability that we must maintain throughout the global government.

"If the judiciary finds grounds for removal, the House and Senate will then bring forward five candidates for election to the vacant office. This process must start within twenty-four hours after the dismissal. The new election process must start within forty-eight hours.

Upon the successful election and confirmation of the president, he or she must take up residence within the compound of the global government headquarters. The president must attend all special meetings of the Senate and the House of Representatives as well as the judiciary branch of government. Special meetings will be deemed those of the utmost importance.

"The Senate will be made up of one elected official from every participating country. These elections will be free elections held for the people and by the people of each and every country. One person is allowed one vote for senator. There will be a permanent base for the Senate. At this time I am very excited to announce that the permanent base for the senators will be in Rome at the site of the ancient Roman Colosseum.

"Even now as I speak, negotiations are underway to rebuild the Colosseum to seat all the senators from around the world. I would like to take this moment to applaud the efforts of the Italian government for meeting the challenge I proposed to them. I have donated all the money necessary for them to rebuild the Colosseum in order to house the senators from around the world. This donation will be made available as soon as confirmation is reached by the Italian government.

"I would also like to thank all the residents of Italy who have stood up and embraced this grand challenge to restore Rome to its past glories of greatness. I hope that the future only brings continued honor and glory upon this great civilization.

"In order for elections to proceed, a census must be taken in each and every country around the world. I will personally employ the census directors in every country around the world responsible for that. They have a very difficult task of counting each and every individual. This is a necessary step in order for elections to begin on a global level.

"Applications will be sent out to those brave enough to accept the challenge of census directors. These directors will be given a budget to hire the necessary people in order to achieve this important step. This will be a huge undertaking, but it's an absolute necessity.

"I would like to pose a challenge to individuals throughout the world. This is your chance to step up and be counted as one. This is also an opportunity to step up and represent your country in a global government that represents everyone on the planet.

"Regardless of how one might feel about politics, do not let this affect the privilege and in this case the absolute right of every individual to accept the calling of their country and become accountable. I realize this is a great responsibility for all, but it is also a great opportunity for those who want a better future for themselves, their children, and their grandchildren.

"The House of Representatives will have their base of operations located in Madrid, Spain. The House of Representatives will also be elected by the population of each country. The number of representatives will be limited by the overall population. For example, one representative will be chosen for all countries with less than one million people. There will also be one representative for special ethnic groups. The second representative will be elected for countries with a population from one to ten million people. The third representative will be elected for a population with ten to a hundred million people. The fourth representative will be elected for populations that range from a hundred million to one billion people. The fifth and maximum number of representatives will have a population more than one billion people.

"This is the reason why a census is so important. We want total accountability for every member of the world's population. Each and every person will be represented in the global government.

"The home for the judiciary branch of the government will be at zero latitude in the great city of London. Negotiations are currently underway in order for a suitable location.

"These are the basics for the birth of the global government. At this time I would like to call on individuals of the media. They are allowed to ask one question with no follow-up questions at this time. My response will be a simple yes or no answer.

"The first question goes to our host country, Greece. What is your question, sir?"

"My name is Gus Zimodus from the *Greek Daily News*. Do you intend to finance the whole initial stages necessary for the global government to function?"

"Yes," I say. "The next question goes to the United States of

America. And if I may take a moment at this time to offer my deepest regrets and condolences to all those lost in a terrible act of aggression that has befallen Washington, DC. Your question, sir?"

"My name is Ted Ruffian from the *New York Daily News*. My question is this. The United States is very skeptical of the timing of your announcements in the wake of the unexplained nuclear disaster on the US Capitol. With all due respect, sir, do you have any information or any knowledge of the bombing that occurred in Washington, DC, or the attempted bombing that occurred near Israel?"

"No," I answer. "The next question goes to the media representative from Italy."

"My name is Joey Altieri from the *Roman Daily News*. Do you plan to tear down the Colosseum and rebuild everything new in its place?"

"No," I say. "The next question will go to the Chinese media representative."

"My name is Michael Wong, and my question is this. If China chose not to become a member of the global government, would any action be taken by the rest of the world to force their participation?"

"No," I say. "The next question will be from the media representative from India."

"My name is Inder Sing from the *New Delhi National Post*. If China refuses membership in the global government, would India then have the most powerful representation within the House of Representatives?"

"Yes," I answer. "The next question is from the representative from South Africa."

"My name is Jackie Beauport from the *South African Post*. Could the whole continent of Africa be represented as one nation in the global government?"

"No," I say. "The next question is from the media representative from the United Kingdom."

"My name is Tim Causeway from the *London Times*. My question is this. If London is chosen as the site for the judiciary branch of the global government, will it remain a permanent site?"

"Yes," I say. "The next question goes to the country of Canada."

"My name is Jack Dancer from the *Montréal News*. Is there any reason why there are no branches of the government located in North America?"

"No," I say. "The last question is from the media representative from Spain."

"My name is to Jesus Alvarez from the *Madrid Daily News*. My question is this. Will you build a new compound to house the House of Representatives?"

"Yes," I answer and then sigh. "This concludes the question-and-answer portion of the speech. In closing, I would like to say that I hope there is very little confusion about the aim of the global government.

"In the next speech, I will discuss more about the three main branches of government. I will also reveal any updates on the current events and progress of the global government.

"The third speech will be located in Rome at the Colosseum in two days' time. Further invitations will be extended to various media organizations from around the world. Additional invitations will be sent to prominent leaders from around the world. I hope that everyone will participate and meet me in Italy.

"I have viewed today as a monumental stride for the individuals with the courage to step forward into the uncertainty of this new frontier. I find serenity, knowing that each step we take brings mankind closer to living in the kind of world our grandchildren will be proud to inherit.

"A world full of hope and opportunity, void of the insurgency that has plagued humankind for a long part of its history. A world free from the threat of war, hunger, and poverty. This world is within our grasp, and we only need the courage to step forward and become accountable.

"In closing, this concept of supreme order will be made much clearer in the speeches that I have prepared for the future. I would like to take this opportunity to thank all those who have attended this speech. I would like to thank Athens for their hospitality over the past couple days. I would also like to thank those of you listening and watching. I hope that you will continue to do so in the future. Thank you very much, and I will see everyone in Rome."

I wave and exit the stage to a loud round of applause. I am escorted to a large limousine, which will take me to the airport where my jet is fueled and waiting.

I seat myself in the back of the limousine. I look over at Ms. Waters and smile. She reaches out her hand. I grab a piece of paper. It reads that an urgent invitation has been scheduled to meet with government representatives from the United States in Las Vegas in about seventy-two hours.

Before the wheels retract under the belly of my jet, Ms. Waters books us the presidential suite in Caesars Palace. She has also assembled my team of lawyers to meet me there. They don't get such luxury settings.

"Ms. Waters, please postpone my next speech by one week. I'll leave the particulars up to you. Use corporate business or something along those lines as my reason for the unexpected postponement."

"Yes, sir, I will handle it," she says.

"I am going to begin preliminary work on the next speech," I say, and Ms. Waters just looks at me.

"What did you think of the presentation of my second speech?" I ask her.

"I didn't think it was good. I thought it needed more polishing.

There was too much technical information. Also, you answered too many questions."

"By all means, don't hold back. Give it to me straight," I say.

"I think I just did. That's what you pay me for, right? To be honest?" she says with a straight face.

"That I do. That I do." I then continue, "I will work on that. Thank you. And another thing—I'm going to make you laugh before this trip is over. Let's have some fun in Vegas. We've earned it."

"You're the boss," she says without smiling.

I get up and move to my sleeping quarters on the jet. The fully enclosed sleeping area is soundproof so I don't have to hear the noisy jet engines, which provides great comfort.

Before I sleep, I check my laptop for messages from Stu. I respond to his concerns. I think about my next speech. I feel my mind wandering, and I can't concentrate. I turn out the lights and sleep.

CHAPTER 14

Agents Blanchard and Davis arrive in Los Alamos, New Mexico, after a short flight from Peterson Air Force Base.

We are met at the airport by Dr. Socorro. He is the head of DARPA, which is responsible for the development of emerging technologies for use by the US military.

I notice that Dr. Socorro is a man of few words. Apart from saying hello, he hasn't spoken a word. He is an older gentleman with long white hair. I can tell he doesn't get out much. His suit is black and aged. He has a blue shirt on with no tie. He's probably enjoying his trip to and from the airport.

I decide to break the silence. "Dr. Socorro, I would like to take this opportunity to say this meeting must remain in the strictest of confidence."

He looks over at me and puts his finger to his lips and makes a shushing sound at me. I remain silent for the rest of the ride.

The three of us walk into DARPA's highly secure building. When we are in a briefing room, Dr. Socorro says, "Sorry about the lack of communication, gentlemen. National security and all that, you understand."

Davis and I nod our heads.

"I have taken the liberty of checking your credentials, gentlemen. The two of you have a higher security clearance than

I do. I understand you would like a crash course on quantum technology, is that right?" Dr. Socorro says.

Davis and I nod our heads again. His lack of communication seems to be contagious.

"All right. I'm not an expert in the field, but I know a little something," he says.

I look over at Davis and squint my eyes as if to say, "Did he just try to make a joke?"

"Gentlemen, I will give you an overview. If you can grasp the general principles without your head exploding, I have a meeting set up with Dr. Gatson and Dr. Reed. They are the experts in the field."

I know he was trying to make a joke that time. I say, "All right, Doctor. We're all ears in a quantum sort of way." I try a joke, but he doesn't laugh.

"Nice try. I've heard them all, quantumly speaking. The detailed explanations that are necessary may take some time. I not here to do that. In order to have a complete grasp of the theoretical intricacies necessary to make clear and educated hypotheses of quantum technology, you have to undergo years of study. I'm not your man for that either," the doctor says. "What I am here to do is give you the basics. Now please listen carefully."

***

Somehow, we get through the basics. We spend long hours with Dr. Gatson and Dr. Reed. We both take detailed notes and record all of the conversations with the experts to review later.

We must have spent about twelve hours at the facility, receiving a crash course on quantum theory. Dr. Socorro kindly gives us a ride back to the airport. I don't know about Davis, but my head is about to explode. None of us talk on the way to the airport. We thank the doctor, and he drives off with a smile and a wave.

I can't wait for our next destination—Vegas. I set up our interview there for a reason.

I spend the short flight to Las Vegas sleeping. I don't know what Davis did. He probably studied notes, knowing him. We land at Las Vegas International Airport. We catch a cab to Caesars Palace, not talking much. I think our brains were overstimulated in New Mexico. We will need time to rest, study, prepare our questions, and perfect our overall strategy. But time is one thing we are short on.

CHAPTER 15

Ms. Waters and I arrive in Las Vegas as the sun begins to set over the mountainous desert ranges. I notice that sunsets in the desert are among the most beautiful anywhere in the world. Streaks of orange and yellow in a background of hot pink with just a hint of green makes this sunset even more exceptional.

We clear customs and take a short cab ride to Caesars Palace. We check in, and we are escorted to our suite on the top floor.

The bellhop says, "Would you like me to show you around your suite, sir?"

I hold out my hand and tip him. "No, thank you."

As he closes the door, he says, "Enjoy your stay."

"I'm sure we won't." I see Ms. Waters off to the side chuckle just a bit. I continue, "I wasn't being racist, was I? Okay, I'll stop being so racism." Ms. Waters starts laughing. I knew I could make her laugh.

She says, "You win. Now stop it."

"All right, let's get some rest. We can hit the town later."

"Good idea, funny man."

***

I have scheduled a late dinner and meeting with my lead lawyer, Mr. Devine. Ned Devine is an incredible corporate law attorney.

I have paid him many millions of dollars in fees each year. He is a large man to say the least. His suits have to be tailored specially for him because they don't make sizes that big off the rack. He is a jolly fellow. He reminds me of Santa Claus in a top-dollar Armani. His laugh bellows around a room. There is no mistaking him in a crowd.

Ms. Waters and I are seated in the world-renowned Mesa Grill at Caesars. I order us three margaritas. Ned is always on time. Just as our server brings our beverages, I hear a bellowing laugh. I know in an instant who it is. He spots us and laughs again. I can't help but smile as I offer him a seat.

Ned says, "Good evening, Dr. H. How you been?"

I say, "Ned, you know I don't like to be called that."

Ned responds, "With a last name like Hornswoggle, you sure ought to." He lets out another loud laugh.

"All right, Ned. You know Ms. Waters."

"Oh, the lovely Ms. Waters. Yes, indeed. The pleasure is all mine. How are you this fine desert evening?" Ned says and then laughs again.

Always the professional, Ms. Waters just nods and smiles.

Ned takes a large gulp of his beverage. "Thanks for the flavored ice, Doc." Then he laughs again.

If this man wasn't the best lawyer in the world, I would fire him just for his laugh. I respond, "Don't laugh, Ned. Your pickin' up the check, you bellowin' buffoon."

He laughs anyway and says, "I like your American accent, Doc. It suits you. Speakin' of suits, how do ya like mine? Twenty-five grand for this."

"I could fit two of me in there, but I wouldn't wanna try. Trust me," I say.

"Of course, I trust ya, Doc. Just as long as your checks don't bounce," he says and laughs.

"All right, Ned. Let's get down to business."

"Right. Business. First thing's first. Did you order dinner?" he says.

Just as he finishes that sentence, our waitperson comes to the table and takes our order. He then begins to summarize the proceedings as he sees them unfolding. I remain speechless. I only listen to the brilliance of the man who is well worth every penny I pay him. When Mr. Devine concludes his soliloquy, I want to give him a standing ovation. Of course, I don't. His head is big enough. Ms. Waters is content to remain silent, probably out of fear of one of Ned's bad jokes. Again, as he finishes, our meals is served. I think he timed that too.

I say, "Excellent, Ned. Just bring that confidence and guidance with you in the morning. You know where the meeting is, right?"

"Of course, Doc. This isn't my first rodeo, ya know," he says and laughs.

"Fine. Finish up, and get your big southwest ass to bed," I say. With a mouthful of food, he says, "Okay, Doc."

***

I wake up and go to the balcony outside. There was a spectacular light show in progress—not from the lights below but from the sky above. Dark purples and black give way to oranges, yellows, and blues. I realize at that moment I could never be just another face in the crowd. I feel inside that a historical change is about to happen.

I have been under scrutiny many times before. I am a confident man who is not affected by stressful situations. I prepare myself. Nothing will impede my greatness.

Ned is a safety net. Nothing will jeopardize the massive gains the company has recently made. I quietly return to the room and head to the shower to get ready. At 8:00 a.m., I begin to make my way to the front desk. I ask the attendant if there are any messages for Dr. Hornswoggle.

He has a smirk on his face at first. I stare him dead in the eyes and squint. He wipes that look off his face in a hurry. He says, "Yes, sir, just one. You are in boardroom A-1. Shall I have someone show you the way?"

I turn and walk away without saying another word. I head to the boardroom. It's about ten after eight. Within moments I approach the large wooden door, and I can hear laughing. I know who is in there. I push through and immediately extend my hand to greet two men in black suits, white shirts, and black ties.

This is going to be a walk in the park. Men in black, how American. They'll be chasing aliens before this meeting is over.

***

I introduce myself and my partner, Agent Davis. We shake hands and sit down, and I start talking.

"Dr. Hornswoggle, can you begin by telling us what you know about quantum physics?" I say. I knew this was an open-ended question, but I thought I would hit him right in the mouth.

He began on a level that seemed understandable at first. It was soon evident, however, that this area of science was anything but understandable.

He says, "The quantum channel is an extremely precious resource, and efforts must be made to enhance and develop that which may become an invaluable and necessary ally."

I say, "Would you care to clarify that statement?"

His lawyer taps him on the shoulder and whispers in his ear. He says, "No, not at this time, gentleman."

"All right, please continue," I says.

"Quantum mechanics is generally agreed upon to be a new field of study. It is hampered by technical limitations that have as yet been unresolved. With Einstein's discovery of quantum energy, a whole new era of study and development has opened up."

"Are you saying that your company is only in the research and development stage?"

"The practical use of this application may someday be used in a global communications arena. The vast percentage of my company's research has dealt with only one aspect of quantum energy," he says.

I ask, "And what would that be?"

His lawyer again taps him on the shoulder and whispers in his ear. "I'm sorry, but to divulge that information would be tantamount to giving away corporate secrets."

"All right," I say. "Without giving away any of your corporate secrets, can you continue to discuss quantum energy?"

His lawyer again whispers. I'm starting to get irritated with this lawyer. I'll probably have to hand this conversation off to Davis soon.

He says, "The field of study with regard to quantum energy is called quantum key distribution. Gentlemen, if you don't understand what I'm talking about, I can back up for you."

"No, please continue. I find this subject fascinating."

He does without any interference from his lawyer. "This field of study is the utilization of the most critical feature of quantum theory. There are only a precise number of directions quantum energy can move in, even though the energy can be in two places at once. Have I lost you?"

"Yes, you lost me on that one. Davis, would you like to give it a go?"

Dr. H squints his eyes and seems taken aback by my verbal queue to Davis. *Hit 'em hard, Davis*, I think.

"Umm, Doctor? You seem to have an excellent understanding of key distribution. Can you tell me a little about that?"

His lawyer leans in. Dr. H nods. I hear him say, "It's okay."

He continues, "Key distribution is limited in its application. This exclusive application is still stunted in its development and application. High-level government agencies and businesses have progressed very little in this area of study. My company included."

"I see. So you're saying that your company is only at the research and development stage then? Is that correct?" I say, baiting him.

"Yes, that's correct."

I continue quickly, "At what frequency does quantum energy operate?"

He starts, "A high—" His lawyer grabs him by the shoulder and whispers in his ear. He continues, "A higher frequency than most communications, but quantum energy is not limited to high frequencies."

"It isn't? What are its limitations then … with regard to frequencies?"

He puts his hand up to his lawyer as if to say, "I will field this question." "My company is only in the research and development stage, so I really wouldn't know the answer to that question."

"You don't know. Are you telling me that I stumped you on a question about quantum energy and how it behaves? C'mon, Doctor. You don't expect me to believe that, do you?"

He just stares at me.

His lawyer speaks up and says, "All right, gentlemen. I think we're done for now. If you would like to talk to my client further, it will be through me. We can see where you're going with this, and it's not going to work. My client has done nothing wrong. He has helped your nation upgrade its low-grade communication system, and now you are attacking him because you can't understand how it works. Good day, gentlemen."

"Good day, gentlemen, and thank you for your time, Doctor," Davis concludes.

The two men leave in a hurry. I look over at Blanchard and say, "You're lucky I studied on the plane while you slept. Well, what do you think? Is this our man?"

Blanchard thinks hard for several moments and then says, "Well, we don't have conclusive evidence. He's arrogant—that's for sure. But I have a gut feeling that this is our man."

I say, "I think you're right."

He says, "Let's go try your hand at blackjack, and test our luck. C'mon. Let's go. It'll be fun."

"No, no, no, and no," I say. "I'm calling the guys from New Mexico. All of us are meeting the president in the morning. And guess what. You're doing the talking, genius."

"Ya know, Watson, I hate it when you go by the book. But damn, you did good! See, my plan worked."

I respond by saying, "These are the evil forces at work! There's no limit to the evil he can do."

Blanchard responded, "I know. I'm not stupid."

CHAPTER 16

At exactly 7:00 a.m., President Gunman walks into the briefing room. I am surprised to see that the president looks aged slightly in such a short period of time.

We all stand. Pat, Commander Sheridan, Director Ryan, Davis, and the two men from New Mexico are all present. When everyone is seated, I begin the briefing. "Mr. President, after much research and investigative procedures, we feel that we have come to several conclusions with regard to the attacks. In order to present these conclusions, we must first explain how we came to them in order for you to fully understand our reasoning.

"As you know, Mr. President, several scientists say that quantum computers are at least five years away. We will dispel that prediction and present evidence to the contrary. We will begin with a brief synopsis of quantum physics and associated concepts. It will become clear that a basic knowledge of quantum physics is necessary. More specifically, we will also attempt to explain photonics, as this study relates to quantum communications.

"Quantum techniques use photons of light to transmit information. Therefore, only light media such as optical fiber or satellite transmissions can only be used when dealing with quantum techniques.

"Wireless networks work in local areas and rely on repeaters and amplifiers to maintain the optical signal. This is not an option for quantum communications, as the repeater must read the signal, which destroys the photon polarization. This process undermines the power of the communication.

"Satellite transmission is the only feasible alternative that we shall explore. At the Los Alamos national laboratory in New Mexico, successful transmissions have been performed up to forty-five kilometers on a clear night."

"The team at Los Alamos has scheduled its first quantum-to-mitigation satellite, and it is to launch in the very near future. The challenge for this team of researchers will be in maintaining the photon polarization strength over great distances.

"While classical mathematical cryptographic functions seem to be sufficient to protect the top-secret data, there is a serious concern that an advanced quantum computer communications satellite will be able to store communications. It will also be able to decrypt them in the future when computers have advanced sufficiently.

"One of the benefits of the new satellite prototype is that it can detect an eavesdropper in the mode of attack. It is possible that they may be able to gain launch codes for nuclear missiles or statistical information on an opponent's military actions.

"Mr. President, we believe that a quantum computer does exist and is currently in place within satellites orbiting Earth. We also conclude that the quantum computer is capable of decrypting all the classical mathematical encryption techniques we currently use. We believe that this is being accomplished through satellite transmissions.

"Satellites are able to repeat the necessary transmissions many times over. They could intercept and decode and then retransmit any information they obtain after analysis. The results could be utterly catastrophic.

"It's our belief that these special communications satellites are responsible for the nuclear attacks. We also think we know who is responsible for the attacks.

"Special Agent Davis will brief you on who we think is behind the missile attacks. Before I turn everything over to him, are there any questions for me at this time, Mr. President?"

There is a brief pause, and there's a look of great concern on the President's face. "Agent Blanchard, am I to believe that a self-aware computer decoded all our most sensitive information? And it has total control of our whole arsenal of nuclear weapons?"

"Yes, sir, Mr. President, not only is our country at grave risk, but other countries are as well."

The president seems shocked. He covers his face with his hands. He then thrusts his hands down on the table. The president says, "Mr. Blanchard, do we know which satellites are equipped with this quantum technology?"

I answer, "We do, Mr. President. We have come to the conclusion that there are four satellites in orbit. Our signal intelligence just confirmed this an hour ago. The computer signals transmit in a high frequency."

The president smiles and says, "Good work, Agent Blanchard."

"If there are no more questions, I'll turn the briefing over to agent Davis.

"Proceed," the president says.

***

I begin, "Thank you, Mr. President. Our investigation has led us to one conclusion. The company responsible is StereoOpticon. I will explain why."

"Current laws don't regulate the exchange of quantum technology or materials used for quantum communications. There are a couple companies here in the United States and overseas that are involved in the development of quantum technology and communications." This area of research and development is very expensive. It is also very time-consuming.

"DARPA has been a leader in the field of study. A prototype quantum transmitter is almost ready for launch. They have spent billions of dollars to get this far in development. We have ruled out any companies here or abroad save one. We have ruled out the Russians and the Chinese. No signals with high frequencies have been detected in either of these countries according to our signal intelligence. Mr. President, we believe there is only one logical conclusion to our investigation.

"Agent Blanchard and I met and interviewed Dr. H in Las Vegas while his lawyer was present. The information we took from this meeting aided us in reaching our conclusion."

The president says, "Excellent work, gentlemen."

"Thank you, Mr. President. As you know, he is on a current campaign to organize and construct a global government. This further strengthens the case we have compiled against him. We must stop him before he becomes the most powerful and wealthiest man on the planet. We do not currently have the necessary physical evidence to be 100 percent confident that Dr. H is behind the two nuclear intrusions."

"Leave that to me, Agent Davis," the president says.

"Yes, sir. Mr. President, we have invited the leading research scientists in this field to attend this briefing to further explain some of the concluding factors to our investigation. If there aren't any more questions, with your permission, may I introduce Dr. McGregor Reed. He is presently the leading scientist in the quantum field of study. He is also the leading adviser to the quantum space division at NASA."

***

"Mr. President, it is an honor," I say.

"The privilege is all mine at the moment, Dr. Reed," the president says with gratitude in his voice.

"That's very kind of you, sir. Mr. President, I have come up with a plan to obtain the necessary physical evidence vital to this case. As I see it, there is only one way to obtain the necessary evidence and bring this man to his knees."

"And that would be a mission to space," the president says.

"Precisely," I respond.

"There's risk involved. And much training is needed prior to launch," the president says.

"The process involves the use of two manned missions with space shuttles launched almost simultaneously. This, of course, would take additional time and training. My estimate to complete the entire mission is approximately two months."

"Dr. Reed, we don't have two months to spare."

"Pardon me, Mr. President," I say. "I think we do, and I will tell you why. Dr. H is currently on a quest to become a leading global politician. I do not think he will risk further disruption to the world's stability and security."

"You have a point," he says.

I continue, "If we utilize every available man working around the clock, we may achieve success in a shorter period of time. But I don't think time is our enemy in this situation. The failure of our mission outweighs any time delays to a massive degree. I have put together a plan for the necessary and proper procedures."

"Dr. Reed, the legal ramifications involved in a mission such as this could have the international court debating its validity for years to come," the president says with a look of skepticism.

"Precisely our aim, Mr. President, not to mention taking out the most powerful weapon mankind has ever seen. There really is no choice in this situation. With all due respect, sir."

The president takes a deep breath, holds it for a moment, and then exhales. He takes another breath and then says, "I believe you are correct, and I am in full agreement. Is there anyone in this room that has any concerns they would like to voice now because now is the time to voice them."

I look around, but no one speaks up.

"Well then, Dr. Reed, you may proceed. I will need a complete report," the president says with a slight smile.

"Thank you, sir," I say.

"And as of this moment, you have all the resources you need and the power to oversee the entire mission until such time as I see fit," the president concludes.

"Thank you, Mr. President."

***

"Commander Sheridan, do you have an update for me?" I ask.

"Yes, Mr. President. About 50 percent of our naval forces are in their home ports. The rest of the fleet will be home in five days. I have ordered patrols just inside international waters about eight miles from our coastline in the Pacific and the Atlantic. About 50 percent of our army, marines, and air force have returned home as well," the admiral says.

"Good. I want you to leave a skeleton crew at our air bases, army posts, and marine stations throughout the world. I want the excess of soldiers to be deployed to Kennedy Space Center. I want to set up a massive tent city around Kennedy Space Center."

"Of course, Mr. President," Commander Sheridan said.

"For security reasons, we must keep this particular mission a secret. The only people who are to know about this mission are the people in this room. Only information necessary to complete specific aspects of this mission may be made available to those involved," I say. "Director Ryan, do you have anything for me?"

"Yes, Mr. President, I have reviewed the vetting process with regard to Dr. H. Director Nichols cleared StereoOpticon. He noted that they were the best equipped company to upgrade our communications network. He said they posed no national security threat and stamped his approval."

"We haven't located the former director, have we?" I ask.

"No, sir. I have implemented new policies throughout the CIA. This type of incident will never slip through the cracks again. I have a full report for you. I also have a copy of the new policy procedures that I have put into effect," the director says.

"Thank you. You can leave those with me."

Everyone says, "Thank you, Mr. President," and we all get up to leave after that.

I say, "Pat, will you meet me in my office?"

He says, "Yes, Mr. President."

"Have a seat, Pat. I will let the American people know about this mission when the time is appropriate. Prior to my announcement, the utmost secrecy is vital to our mission."

"Of course, Zac. We will use only encryption-capable communications. I will have a signal intelligence group placed in Central Florida. They will control and monitor all calls made within the area. They will block any attempts to make any outside calls," Pat says.

"Excellent," I say. "Pat, I wanted to talk to you about Carol. She's still in an induced coma. I haven't heard from any doctors in days."

"Say no more, Zac. I will get on the horn and take care of it for you."

"Thanks, Pat. You know I would do it myself, but I can't keep calling the hospital every hour and make everyone jump. I know they are caring for an unbelievable amount of patients."

"I will update you as often as I can," Pat says.

"All right," I say. "Let's get back to work."

CHAPTER 17

I am ready to deliver the third speech. A stage is set up in front of the Colosseum. As I exit the limo, I hear the huge crowd that has assembled begin to clap and cheer. I wave in acknowledgment and shake hands with everyone I can on my way to the podium. I raise my hands, and the crowd settles down.

"I would like to start out by saying welcome to everyone here in attendance and those of you watching around the world. A special thanks is extended to the Italian government for their complete cooperation and assistance in a reconstruction process involved with the Colosseum. I am delighted to announce that work has begun to restore the Colosseum to its former grandeur."

The crowd erupted in cheers.

"I must also report that census directors have been put in place around the world. They are using current statistical information, and they are beginning the task of counting everyone in the world. I would like to thank them in advance and remind them that time is of the essence.

"I know many people have questions, so I'd like to begin today by fielding some questions. But before I do, I would like to explain briefly how the Senate will function.

"Elections will take place every ten years. They will live and work here in Rome. Senators may bring legislation forward to be voted on, and a majority is needed to pass any legislation. I will go into more detail on the different committees in the Senate at a later date. At this time, I would like to field some questions.

"The first question goes to the media representative from Moscow. Your question, sir?"

"My name is Yuri Pacheco of the *Moscow Daily News*. My question is this. How do countries gain membership to the global government?"

"Membership is automatic and open to all countries. All that is needed is confirmation that the countries will participate in the census-gathering stage. There is no cost to participate in the global government," I say. "The next question goes to the representative from Spain."

"My name is Carlos Sanchez from the *Spanish Gazette*. If there is no cost to any country, how will the global government sustain itself over a period of many years?"

"I will set up an initial fund of ten billion dollars. This money will be invested by a committee whose sole task is making money to sustain the government. Another committee will check the progress on a daily basis. Great importance will be placed on financial operations," I say. "The next question goes to the representative from Israel."

"My name is Mark Haussler. While we're on the subject of finances, how much will all the members of each branch be paid, and what type of hours will they work?"

"That is an excellent question. All members of the House of Representatives, Senate, and judiciary branch as well as the president will receive an annual salary of $52,000 per year. All the members will work fifty weeks a year. This is a full-time task. There will not be a day in the year that the government is not operating. There will be no official holidays; however, representatives from each country will have the right to observe special holidays that are specific to their country or culture.

"If people think that they will get rich by becoming representatives for their country, they will be mistaken. These positions are not about becoming rich or famous. These positions have to become your life's mission. Only 100 percent dedication will yield success. Everyone involved must put forth their greatest effort if we are to achieve our greatest goals," I say. "The next question goes to the media representative from Iraq."

"My name is Haddam Hussein. How is this global government different from the United Nations?"

"There will be no threat of force used to achieve any desired results, not like the way the United Nations uses powerful countries and the threat of military force to achieve its goals. The United Nations and the World Trade Organization will become obsolete in time. I know this may sound a bit radical to most of you. This global government will achieve success through legislation and worldwide cooperation. Disputes will be settled in governmental chambers, not on the battlefield. There will become no need for terrorist activities because a balance of power throughout every country around the globe will exist.

"No country will be more powerful than the next in this government. One of the most important goals of the global government is to eliminate any need for war. This includes terrorist activities.

"The United States is currently in a war against terrorism. It is a battle that they will lose. A country cannot fight an ideology or a religion. There is no winner on either side. The losers are only the innocent lives that are lost because of the terrorist attacks and the retaliations of those countries that are attacked by the terrorists.

"Terrorists have no names, no countries, no accountability for their actions. Any man, woman, or child can become a terrorist.

Terrorists have no goals, no agendas except to instill fear in others and bring about Armageddon. Life on earth is far too short to live in constant fear of others. Even the most powerful military country or coalition can never defeat terrorism or terrorist activities."

"There is no battlefront, no firing line that is defined, and no specific enemy that can be identified. We must remove the need for terrorism in order to defeat it," I say. "The next question goes to the representative from New Zealand."

"How will the global government benefit small countries?"

"Every country in the world has something to offer that will benefit others. Even New Zealand has something to offer the rest of the world. New Zealand has arguably the best lamb and sheep in the world. Why shouldn't they be allowed to export to every country around the world without being taxed. Trade routes will flourish around the world. Food will get to every individual around the world, limiting hunger and eliminating starvation. People should be allow to trade food items freely amongst countries.

"This is another major goal of the global government— to eliminate hunger and starvation worldwide through greater cooperation and sound international legislation between all the countries of the world. I'm not saying that this goal will be an easy one to obtain. Through hard work and cooperation, it will be achieved. How can we as an intelligent people call ourselves civilized if we allow hunger and starvation to exist?

"For example, the people who choose to live in the extremes of the African desert call this place their home. If given the opportunity, these people could cultivate desert cacti and export their products around the globe. Their tourist industry would flourish if no hostilities existed. There are other products they could export as well. They can then import all the food they need to survive.

"The global government will also have a business and trade

committee to help facilitate cooperation. They will establish new trade routes around the world. Once this has been accomplished, there is no reason why the world couldn't operate on a single currency, making all of these countries equal. We all live in one world. There should be no distinction between first, second, or third worlds," I say. "The next question goes to the Democratic Republic of Congo situated in Central Africa."

"My name is Dizembe Mutombo from the *Kinshasa Gazette*. My question is this. When people speak about Africa, they speak of it as a whole country with individual states, much the same as the United States. Why then can Africa not be counted as one country?"

"Most people say that China is the sleeping giant of the world. I say that Africa has the potential to be the awakened giant in the world. Africa is undergoing internal strife, disease, famine, and civil war. Until Africa can unite and become stable as one country, it cannot be considered a country as a whole such as the United States.

"Even the United States went through civil war, but it has emerged as a united country and has blossomed to become an economic leader.

"I see a bright future for Africa as a major contributor to the global economy. This region has great potential. Africa has unique wildlife, flora and fauna, and a spirit for survival that is unmatched by any country in the world.

"We must tap into these resources. Africa is centrally located, and it has much to offer. It can become the center of global trade routes, a sort of staging point to all the world's trade. However, until Africans can obtain stability in their continent, Africa will run in knee-high mud while other countries will gallop on firm ground.

"At this time, I must end the questions, but in one week I will give another speech in Madrid. I thank all of the thousands of people who have attended today and look forward to seeing you all and many new faces in Spain. I thank you all for your attention, and I look forward to explaining in more detail the essence of the global government. I'll see everyone next time in Madrid."

The crowd begins a thunderous applause. I exit the stage and shake hands with as many people as possible. My limo is waiting. I jump inside quickly. I look over at Ms. Waters and ask, "Well, how did I do this time?"

"Well, better with the technical aspect but—"

"But?" I say.

"But your answers to the questions are too long-winded. I think you started to lose some people. You need to be more concise and to the point without explaining everything all the time," she says.

"You're right. I'll work on that. Thank you."

"You're welcome. Can we get some dinner at a nice restaurant? I'm starved."

"Of course," I say. "I already made reservations."

"You actually made reservations? Now I'm impressed," she says with a smile.

"Was that a joke, Ms. Waters? Very good."

"Well, you know what they say. When in Rome—"

"Yep, let's do it like they did in Roman times."

"Don't get cheeky," she says.

"No, ma'am, not me."

CHAPTER 18

Seventy-two hours has passed since I met with the president. I feel the need to gather everyone involved in the upcoming mission. I take my place at the podium to address several thousand people standing in front of me.

I begin, "NASA employees and more importantly, everyone who has been invited to partake in our most recent endeavor, I stand before you this morning in what is the dawn of our greatest challenge put forth by the president of the United States.

"Make no mistakes about this, ladies and gentlemen. This challenge surpasses the one that President Kennedy made when he declared that the United States would be the first nation to set foot on the moon.

"The triumphant return of the crippled Apollo 13 mission pales in comparison to the undertaking that we are about to embark on. The dangers are greater than those faced by the courageous men and women who we shall never forget in the space shuttle *Columbia*. There is a great chance that people will lose their lives during this mission.

"President Gunman has presented us with the ultimate challenge, a challenge that is like no other presented before us in the whole history of the NASA program. We do not get any second chances with this mission, ladies and gentlemen.

"The words 'failure' or 'cannot be done in time' are not words that any of us can utter from this moment forward. Positive thinking is the allowable kind now, and anyone who feels that they may have a problem with this is advised to remove themselves now. I will not tolerate any negative thinking at any point in time. This is your only warning.

"The future existence of the United States of America depends on this. I cannot divulge all the specific details at this moment in time. All will be revealed in due time.

"What is most important now is that everyone in this hangar must be in the correct frame of mind before we begin our tasks, which will start immediately after this briefing. With that being said, I will now begin an outline of what is going to happen and what must be done.

"It is now everyone's duty as American citizens to concentrate on what I am going to tell you and also to begin to formulate a plan and how this mission can best be achieved in the shortest amount of time.

"What follows are the general guidelines that make up the essence of our mission. Firstly, we are going to launch two space shuttles simultaneously. We'll be on similar missions. We must make both space shuttles fully operational within twenty-one days. Before anyone raises the issue that this is not possible, I will tell you that additional manpower will become available in the very near future. It is your sole responsibility to concentrate on the objective at hand. You must trust in yourself and others that we will meet this goal on time.

"In approximately three weeks, NASA will conduct a dual launch of space shuttles *Enterprise II* and *Columbia II*. Launches will occur almost simultaneously from here at Kennedy Space Center.

"Mission control in Houston will monitor and control both

launches from their headquarters. They are making preparations in order to fulfill their portion of the mission. I have every confidence that Houston will succeed when blastoff begins.

"Each of you has been handed general orders that pertain to your department of operation. I will expand on these orders in the form of a general overview of what each of you can expect in the coming weeks.

"The training must be expanded for each and every department and tailored to each category of training. The twelve most elite astronauts will undergo extensive training during this period. There will be six backup astronauts training for this mission as well.

"The training regime will be grueling and extensive. Everyone has been assigned to specific teams. I need everyone to review the information and get back to me as soon as possible with what they need in order for this mission to be successful. We have at our disposal all the resources we need for this particular mission. When making recommendations for personnel and equipment, do not hesitate to request everything that is necessary. Our number-one priority is the success of this mission, and nothing else matters.

"I want everyone to break up into their groups in order to conduct your initial analysis. I want any request on my desk by noon. The request will include anything that you need with regard to manpower and equipment or anything else that is necessary in order for you to fulfill your part of the mission.

"The president is watching, ladies and gentlemen. The rest of the country is relying on us. There is no room for error.

"I will have an open-door policy if there are any problems. Anyone who feels that they are not up to this may approach me in my office. I hope that everyone will put forth 100 percent of their efforts into this extremely important mission. And remember, I am not your boss. The president of the United States is your boss on this mission."

CHAPTER 19

The Learjet with me and Ms. Waters lands in Madrid without any incident. I am whisked away by limousine to the posh living quarters at the Hotel Madrid. I continue to work on the next speech, going over it in my mind. I feel I am well prepared to shock the world. I am confident but not arrogant about beginning the process of initiation of the global government.

We rest for the evening, and we have a bite to eat. Then I get ready for my fourth speech. I hope this speech is better than my last.

At exactly noon my limousine pulls up in front of the Plaza de Toros de las Ventas. This is the location of the next speech. It has a seating capacity of twenty-five thousand people, and it is regarded as the home of bullfighting in Spain. It is the perfect location, and the arena is at full capacity with standing room only. I am humbled by my popularity, which has skyrocketed in a short period of time. It's either out of curiosity or genuine interest in what I have proposed to the world.

I make my way to the center of the arena, shaking hands along the way and waving to the crowd as people start cheering. The crowd begins to quiet as I stand at the podium, ready to begin.

"It is a pleasure to be here in Spain with its endless culture and home to the most beautiful people in the world."

The crowd is whipped into a cheering frenzy again, and Spanish flags begin to wave in the massive crowd. The crowd again begins to settle, and a hush takes over the arena in anticipation.

"Let me begin by saying that our hopes and prayers go out to all those people affected by the recent attacks in the United States. Many innocent people have lost their lives. We can only ensure that their lives were not lost in vain.

"I stand before you all today to offer everyone a brighter future. We all can eliminate barbarous acts upon mankind forever."

A huge roar began to build from the exuberant crowd.

"I believe that the global government can change the way people around the world think and act toward one another. I also believe leaders from all nations will begin to realize that they are accountable for all their decisions and actions, their own people as well as those outside their borders.

"I would like to take this opportunity to further define the role and responsibilities of the House of Representatives based here in Madrid. The elections will be held every ten years. Once the final numbers are made public from the census or the projected population program, a specific number of representatives will be assigned to each country or ethnic group. A list of all the countries and their specific number of representatives will be made public very soon. All ethnic groups that are under one million in population will receive one representative.

"I would like to briefly describe the election process. Each country or group can have up to ten names nominated for the House of Representatives.

"I encourage anyone interested to begin to campaign so that you can be one of the ten names to run in the election. Then out of the ten names, the highest vote counts will win the seats available in the House.

"The goal is to make professional politicians who truly believe in what they are doing will make a difference in the lives of everyone around the globe.

"The Senate elections will take place first because there will only be one representative seat available. That election is slated to take place in two weeks, so do not delay if you feel you can make a difference. Campaign now, and get your name on the ballots.

"Family members will be housed and cared for as well. A complex is under construction as we speak here in Madrid for the House of Representatives.

"Madrid should feel proud to host the first sitting of the new global House of Representatives."

A loud roar fills the arena, and people again wave flags. More than twenty-five thousand people begin to yell and scream.

"Committee membership will take on the majority of the workload. Having the right people in the right places is crucial for success. For example, the committee on trade would be one of the largest because of its vital importance. This issue concerns every nation and individual on the planet.

"The committee on global peace will be made up of individuals who have excellent diplomatic and communication skills. These individuals are extremely important to ensure that various cultures coexist peacefully. But there is always common ground because we are all people sharing the same planet.

"Another important committee is the global finance committee. This committee may be made up of bankers, lawyers, stockbrokers, and accountants. There will be no tax base from which to draw money, so this committee is extremely important in order to keep the whole global government operating.

"So you see, there are many important responsibilities that everyone must undertake, and accountability is of the utmost importance.

"There will also be an internal ethics committee to make sure that everyone is accountable for their actions. It is now clear why accountability for one's actions is a necessary function of the House as a whole.

"In closing, it is easy to understand that the global government will evolve and grow over time. This is one of the amazing aspects of the government. Its members will grow, develop, and evolve along with it. The right people will constantly push to achieve its desired goals to benefit mankind.

"I understand that we must first crawl before we walk and walk before we run, but once we begin to run, our achievements are only bound by our imaginations. Nothing will be impossible if we all work together to achieve success.

"I will go more in depth about the functions and responsibilities of the global government in later speeches, but for now we must learn to crawl.

"Thank you for your enthusiasm, your patience, and your participation. I will speak to everyone again very soon."

I wave to the crowd as I exit. Cheers begin again, and I see a sea of smiles looking back at me.

I am whisked away by limo. I am escorted by a police motorcade this time. I look over to Ms. Waters. She has a smile on her face as she looks out her window. Thousands of people have gathered along the street.

I ask, "Well, how did I do this time?"

She looks over at me and says, "Much better. I think your starting to get the hang of it. Always compliment the crowd."

"I see what you mean. Next stop on the whistle tour, London."

CHAPTER 20

I am startled awake by a loud knock on the door. Pat slowly opens the door and softly says, "Mr. President, are you awake?"

"I am now, Pat. What is it?" I respond. *I'll never get used to being woken up in the middle of the night.*

"I have news about the first lady," Pat says in a soft voice.

"That's wonderful news, Pat. Make a pot of strong coffee, will you? I need to freshen up a bit. You can fill me in on the details," I say.

I emerge from the bathroom, feeling more awake, but I'm now concerned. I take long swallow on the hot black coffee. I wave my hand in a gesture so that Pat knows he can begin.

"Zac, I really don't know where to begin, so I'll just start talking. During the evacuation the vice president lost his footing and fell just in front of the blast doors. The first lady was right behind him, and in a reflex action, she grabbed him and tried to pull him to his feet. They both fell in the process, and the first lady hit her head on the concrete. The Secret Service agents pulled them both in the shelter only moments before the impact.

"Both sustained some injuries. The worst was the first lady's though. No one really knows what happened exactly, but the first lady was unconscious when doctors attended to her. They are afraid to move her more than is necessary," Pat says in a somber voice.

I remain silent, taking in the information with disbelief. I'm too shocked to speak.

Pat continues, "Vice-President Sands is now at Peterson Air Force Base and in good health except for a little bump on his forehead. The vice president hit his head and fell backward into the first lady.

"Your brave wife tried to catch him before he went to the ground. They both ended up falling to the concrete floor. The first lady took the worst of the fall. The first lady actually saved the vice president's life, or at the very least, she aided in his safety. The first lady is a hero, Mr. President," Pat says in a dignified tone.

"Thank you for the information, Pat," I say. "I would like to speak to the head doctor as soon as possible. Please make it so."

"Right away, Zac. I will connect the call myself. I will make sure you are not disturbed," he says.

"Thanks, Pat, but who besides you is going to disturb me in the middle of the night?"

"Good point, but you never know, Mr. President," Pat says.

Pat hands me the phone as it begins to ring, and then he heads out the door. I answer in a low voice, "Hello, this is the president. With whom am I speaking?"

The voice on the other end of the line has a serious tone. "This is Dr. Cassidy, Mr. President."

"Hello, Doctor."

"Mr. President, your wife sustained a serious blow to the back of her head as she fell backward with the full weight of the vice president on top of her.

"As you know, we had to induce a coma in order to operate on her cranium to relieve the pressure and swelling of her brain. The operation was successful. She is still in a coma. We are monitoring her progress very closely."

"Thank you, Dr. Cassidy," I say. "I know she is in your capable hands at the moment, but I would like for her to be transported here with me as soon as she is able."

"Yes, Mr. President, as soon as I feel she can be safely transported, I will arrange that for you. I will give you updates on a daily basis and keep you informed of her condition," Dr. Cassidy said without hesitation.

"Thank you, Doctor. I would fly there immediately if her condition worsens, but it would be very difficult for me to leave at this moment. I'm sure you understand why."

"Of course, Mr. President. I understand. I will keep you—"

I can hear a woman's voice in the background on the other end of the line.

"Mr. President, I must go. I will call you back." Then he hangs up.

I hang up the phone, and tears begin to run down my cheeks. I don't want to be here. I want to be by my wife's side. I know the greater good of the country as a whole is a priority. The needs of the many outweigh my needs, but it still hurts.

CHAPTER 21

I am in the office at StereoOpticon two weeks after what I hoped was another successful speech in London. I am watching the election results as they are posted from around the world for the House of Representatives.

The election results have been decided for the Senate. I am preparing letters with committee assignments for the senators. I have given them the task of assigning the members of the House to their committees.

The House of Representatives will soon receive their first duties as members of the global government. It is a proud moment for me, and I hope for them as well.

The Senate members have already chosen and confirmed eleven members for the judicial branch of government.

Most of the major media centers from around the globe are covering the election process. After all, we are making history. Out of chaos, I have created a new global government.

However, the work is not yet done. There is still much to complete still. Now with the elected officials almost in place, my dream will be realized. A new world order will begin to take form. Stability and hope for the future can now begin for every nation involved. Mankind is about to take a giant leap forward in more ways than it could ever imagine, and future generations will remember me as the architect for this society.

I hear a light knock on the door. It must be Ms. Waters. "Come in, Ms. Waters," I say.

"You called for me?" Ms. Waters says in a questioning tone.

"Yes, I would like you to send out an urgent e-mail to all the senators on the confidential server. Instruct them to begin the selection process for the executive branch of government. Tell the senators the deadline is forty-eight hours from now," I say.

"Right away," she says.

"Be sure to let them know I expect no delays, and this is a priority-one message. Thank you, Ms. Waters."

"Yes, sir," she says and then walks quickly through the door to her office.

Within twenty-four hours, the House of Representatives will be in place. The three branches of government will almost be complete after they decide to nominate a president. The next seventy-two hours are going to be as monumental as they are exciting.'

CHAPTER 22

I hear a knock on my office door and wonder, *Who is knocking? Nobody knocks anymore.* I yell, "Come in."

"Zac, I have an urgent call from Dr. Cassidy on my cell." Pat hands me his phone.

"Hello?" I say.

"Mr. President, this is Dr. Cassidy. I'm afraid I have some bad news for you, sir."

"Do I need to fly out to Fairfax?" I said.

"Mr. President, your wife developed a blot clot in her brain, and it dislodged and moved to her heart. We did everything we could to save her. I'm so very sorry, Mr. President."

I drop the cell phone, put my hands over my face, and cry.

***

I wait outside Zac's office for quite some time. I know he knows the rules about no cell phones. I start to think he may be getting some bad news. I decide to knock. I heard a low mumble. I rushed in to make sure the Zac is okay. He is sobbing. I say, "Zac, we can get through this together."

He composes himself a little and says, "Pat, your my best friend, but Carol was the compassion, the face of all things good in this crazy world."

"She's the best, a national hero. We won't let her go in vain. I promise you," I says.

"You were there for me when my parents passed. Can I ask you to be there for me again?" Zac says.

"Always, my friend. I'll take care of everything."

"And Pat, roll out the shuttles. We are go for launch in twenty-four hours. Make it so!" he says with a look of conviction.

Yes, that's the president of the United States we elected. No more hiding in the shadows.

"Yes, sir, Mr. President," I say.

I must call Dr. Reed. The time has come to proceed with the shuttle launches. We have no time to spare. There's so much to do.

The dual shuttle launch to retrieve evidence of the quantum technology from the satellites is at hand. We have been tracking Dr. H's four satellites for weeks now. We will prove that he is behind the nuclear attacks. This is our chance to find out the truth.

CHAPTER 23

I turn on my microphone from Houston to Kennedy Space Center to address everyone involved in the upcoming mission. I begin, "Ladies and gentlemen, our preparation for this unprecedented mission has passed. We now enter the execution phase. Everyone must now concentrate on the mission at hand.

"Remember, success and Godspeed. We now have less than one hour before launch."

I look around at everyone preparing for the launch, and I think about how proud I am to be a part of this mission. I'm especially proud of Colonel Williams and Captain Monroe of *Columbia II* and Colonel Hardy, Captain Getty, and Captain Riley of *Enterprise II*.

The time passes very quickly. It seems like only moments have passed, and then the countdown begins.

The launch protocols are all in place. What remains is the steady countdown toward the launch of the newly refitted and upgraded *Enterprise II* and *Columbia II*.

"Five,four. Fire engines. Three, two, one. Lift off of shuttle *Enterprise II*. Houston, we have lift off of shuttle one," flight lead from Kennedy says.

"Five,four. Fire engines. Three, two, one. Lift off of shuttle

Columbia II. Houston, we have lift off of the first ever dual shuttle launch. Houston, you are in command. Kennedy out!"

"Thank you, Kennedy. This is Houston. We are in command. Over," I say.

"Switching over to secure communications," coms officer McFerran replies.

"Enterprise and Columbia, do you read? This is Flight. Do you copy?"

"This is Enterprise. We copy. Over."

"This is Columbia. We copy. Over."

"This is Flight. Copy that. Coms check. We are now maintaining triple communications for the rest of the mission. It is vital that we maintain coms at all times. I want radio contact from the coms officer at all times. This mission relies on split-second maneuvers. We will guide y'all through every procedure. Just maintain coms. Over."

"Enterprise copies."

"Columbia copies."

"Excellent. Any problems, give us a shout-out. We see what you see for the most part. When we approach the satellites, it becomes mission critical. Then the coms will heat up, and everyone has to be on their toes. Is that a copy?" I say.

"Copy, lead," the captains say over the coms almost in unison.

"Godspeed, gentlemen, and move to one hundred kilometers in trail of designated satellites. We will know when y'all are in position. But relay your confirmation at that point. Copy?" I say.

Two voices respond, "Copy, lead."

The shuttles make it to space without any glitches. Enterprise is moving counter clockwise, and Columbia is moving clockwise with the Earth's rotation. The mission is essential to capture both satellites at the same time on opposite ends of the planet. This will disrupt communications between the other two orbiting satellites, thus effectively shutting down any future communications between the four satellites.

Most importantly, we will capture the satellites for evidence. We will evaluate the satellites and analyze the data. This investigation will lead to the answers President Gunman is seeking.

"Flight lead, this is Columbia ll. We are approaching a hundred kilometers from designated satellite. We are deploying thrusters to slow speed, and we await further orders. Over."

"Copy, Columbia. We have you on radar. Begin video recording and maintain line of sight toward the satellite. Hold at fifty kilometers in trail. Over," I say.

"Copy, Flight," Colonel Williams, the pilot of Columbia, says.

I watch as Columbia maneuvers exactly behind the satellite and holds position, waiting for further orders.

"Columbia, this is Flight. We would like you to slowly move within one kilometer of the satellite. Enterprise is approaching a hundred kilometers from their objective. Over," I say.

"Copy, Flight," Colonel Williams says.

"Flight, this is Enterprise. We are approaching a hundred kilometers from the designated target and deploying thrusters to slow to fifty kilometers in trail," Colonel Hardy, pilot of Enterprise, says.

"Copy, Enterprise. We have you on radar. Continue and trail fifty kilosmeters behind designated target and begin video," I say.

"Copy, Flight," Colonel Hardy says with no hesitation.

"Columbia, move to within two hundred feet of the satellite and hold. Begin preparations for spacewalk and satellite retrieval. Over," I say.

"Copy, Flight. Columbia moving to two hundred feet in trail, and Captain Monroe is ready and waiting in the shuttle bay. Over," Colonel Williams says.

"All right, Columbia. Here we go. Open shuttle bay doors. Deploy Captain Monroe for capture," I order.

I watch as Captain Monroe begins his slow approach tethered by a steel cable—the same cable that will pull him and the satellite back into the shuttle through the bay doors, which are specially designed to fit the entire satellite.

Captain Monroe approaches at a hundred feet from the satellite, and suddenly, a panel slides sideways, exposing the internal workings of the satellite.

With a degree of excitement in his voice, Captain Monroe says, "Flight, are you seeing what's happening on video? A side panel has just—"

Before Captain Monroe can utter another word, a beam of light emanates from the satellite. It hits Captain Monroe and continues toward *Columbia II*. Within seconds, the beam cuts Captain Monroe in half. With the tether cut, his body drifts in two parts away from the satellite. The shuttle sustains extensive damage and explodes in a great fireball. Everyone on board is lost. Parts of the shuttle fly in every direction.

Everyone at mission control in Houston is shocked. I try to speak, but nothing comes out.

I take a deep breath, my heart pounding, adrenalin coursing through my body. My attention turns immediately, and I yell, "Enterprise, hold position. Do not move any closer to target. Do you copy? Over."

"Copy, Flight," Colonel Hardy says.

Dr. Reed takes a few deep breaths and begins to speak to everyone over the loudspeaker in Houston. "We are going to proceed with our backup plan. Everyone, refocus your attention to the tasks at hand."

I'm fully aware that the president is watching the mission from his situation room. He must be extremely worried right about now, but I know the mission is not yet over. There is still hope for success, but time is limited.

Whoever is in control of the satellites will surely know very soon what has happened. The mission just got more complicated and dangerous.

"Enterprise, we are now implementing the secondary plan. Time is of the essence. We are uploading the video of Columbia's mission. Proceed to 250 feet from the satellite. Deploy the dummy spacewalker, and take aim on that panel where that beam of light came from. Have everyone in place and ready at 250 feet from the satellite. Over," I say.

"Copy that, Flight. We have the video, and we are maneuvering into position. Everyone is standing by to implement the secondary plan. Over," Colonel Hardy said without hesitation.

"It's up to your team now, Colonel," I say. But Colonel Hardy already knows.

"Copy that, Houston," Colonel Hardy responds.

The tethered space dummy is deployed from the bay doors, and they aim it directly at the satellite. Captain Getty has his feet firmly planted in the shuttle bay, his gun aimed on the panel, just waiting for movement from the panel door.

As the space dummy approaches about a hundred feet from the satellite, the satellite makes a slight thrust adjustment and rotates a few degrees toward the space dummy. The panel doors begin to slide open at the same moment.

This gives Captain Getty only moments to take aim and shoot out the proximity defense. He fires two rapid shots into the satellite, hoping to disable the proximately defense without doing much damage to the interior of the satellite.

His aim is true, and he hits the device. However, his shot also knocks the satellite slightly off course, and it begins to drift away. The satellite doesn't engage its thrusters to correct its course either .

The Enterprise makes its move and quickly closes in on the satellite for capture. I'm holding my breath, hoping no more defenses remain.

The Enterprise positions itself just below the satellite, and Captain Riley secures it and pulls it into the shuttle with a special tether.

The plan works, and within moments the satellite is safely inside the shuttle. Then they close the bay doors. I know there's still a major worry that the satellite may be equipped with a self-destruct capability.

The crew of the Enterprise quickly goes to work on the satellite. They dismantle it, and they find no self-destruct mechanism, which is a relief.

"Houston, the package has been secured. Are we to initiate destruction of the secondary target?" Colonel Hardy asks.

"Hold position, Enterprise," I say.

Just then my phone rings. I say, "Yes, Mr. President. I understand, Mr. President. Thank you, sir." I hang up after the conversation.

"Return immediately, Enterprise. The president wants your team home safe. Over. And good job," I say.

I feel relieved that it's over. But I can't help feeling that we let the president down. How could we have known that the satellites had defenses? We should have planned for that scenario on the first shuttle approach.

CHAPTER 24

I've been very busy preparing a speech for the newly elected members of the Senate, the House of Representatives, and the judiciary branch. The members have overwhelmingly selected me as the first president of the global government.

The camera crew is in the process of setting up their equipment to record my acceptance speech, and then Ms. Waters enters the office. She walks over to me and whispers in my ear. I look at her. She nods her head.

I say, "You're absolutely positive we have lost a satellite?"

She nods again.

I say, "Get Ballarat up here now! Tell him to realign the three satellites so we can maintain line of sight."

"He's doing that now, she says." She turns and rushes toward the exit.

I move into position to give my acceptance speech, which will be broadcasted to the global government representatives. I have to show great joy. An expression of surprise will be easy.

I begin, "Members of the global government, I would first like to congratulate everyone on being elected to your new positions.

"I graciously accept your appointment to be the first president of the global government. It is a great honor to have earned your respect and admiration, and I thank you."

"I would like to take this time to speak to everyone about the dedication that so many have shown thus far. I am very proud of each individual, and I know everyone will perform to the best of their abilities. I will be accountable for my actions, and I expect the same from every representative of the global government.

"I understand there will be many challenges ahead, but I have the utmost confidence in everyone's abilities to perform their duties. I also understand that some representatives may feel outside pressures from individual state governments. Rest assured that everyone will be kept safe and free from intimidation. Everyone must vote with their conscience. We must consider the best interests of the entire world.

I have a surprise for all of you. For those of you who wish to remain in your own country, I have developed a holographic imageing system. This will allow you to participate in debates on the floor and attendance at committees from the comfort of your home or office. I hope this will alleviate any concerns that you may have about leaveing your countries. This will also serve those who must be in country for emergencies.

"Again, congratulations to you, and I thank you for the awesome responsibility and honor you have bestowed upon me. I shall be on my way very soon to meet with each and every one of you personally. But for now, let's get to work and make the world a place we all can be proud of."

The broadcast ends. I look up from the teleprompter and see Ballarat's face. I become inflamed with rage. I point at him and say, "In my suite now!"

He walks behind me, and we enter my living quarters. I shut the door behind us and say, "Someone has to take the blame for this incompetence. Guess who that is!" He just looks at me, not uttering a word. "You will disappear forever. If you ever resurface, I think you know what will happen to you. You will go to Argentina and have facial surgery. You will not go out in public for two years. Is that clear?"

He nods his head. I yell, "Is that understood?"

He says, "Yes, understood."

"Go! Now!"

CHAPTER 25

I sit at the desk in the made-for-TV room. I look around and realize how phony this looks. Starting tomorrow, I vow that this administration will never broadcast from this location again. I will not hide. I will not be intimidated any further.

I hear the director of communications say, "You're on in five, four, three—" Then he points. I begin, "Good evening, my brave fellow Americans. I would like to take this opportunity to speak to everyone and provide some information on our progress as a nation.

"I will be brief this evening because there is still much work to be done to achieve our desired goals. I am happy to report that the federal government is back up and running. The state governments are returning to normalcy as well.

"The Red Cross has provided help to those in need. Operations are still underway to rescue everyone in the blast zone.

"I would like to take this opportunity to thank everyone for their sacrifices in helping those in need. I am very proud to be a citizen of the United States, and you should be too.

"We continue to work with our allies in order to maintain stability throughout many regions of the world. We will not become an isolationist country. We will not cower in fear. We must stand up and stand together now more than ever.

"We are continuing our investigation into the attack on

Washington, DC, and the attempted attack on Tel Aviv. We have recently acquired new evidence, and the responsible party will be brought to justice very soon. I want to make this point very clear. No one attacks us and gets away with it. No one. We will be forever vigilant and bring those responsible to justice one way or another. This I guarantee.

"I want to reassure everyone that your safety remains the primary concern … and the safety of our nation as a whole. This has been and will always be the top priority.

"I will be addressing the nation again very soon with more updates on our progress. Thank you for your attention. For now, be safe. God bless everyone, and God bless the United States of America."

The broadcast ends, and Pat slowly walks over to me. I say to him, "Pat, let's get the hell out of here."

"I thought you'd never say so. With pleasure, and may we never return to this hole in the mountain again."

"Not while I'm in charge we won't," I say.

"I've already made arraignments," Pat says.

"And Pat, let's go git that son of a bitch."

"I've already made arraignments," Pat says.

"I knew I could count on you."

ABOUT THE AUTHOR

James P. Travers joined the Air Force and worked as an Intelligence Specialist during the Cold War, stationed in Germany. He is a decorated war veteran who participated in Operation Desert Shield/Storm during the Persian Gulf War. He studied political science at Saint Leo University and attended law school at Auckland University in New Zealand.

Printed in the United States
By Bookmasters